Just a Friend

Deb Goodman

Contents

For Lindzee. You are brilliant.

Join Deb's newsletter to get the book, Just a Road Trip: a Sweet, Longdale Lake RomCom, totally FREE!

   https://BookHip.com/LZFLFSX

Chapter 1

Sophie

Oliver Tate is an egotistical jerk and I hate him.

I'm in the outdoor seating area at a milkshake shop—alone. The purple plastic table across from me has an enormous wad of gum stuck under it. I bet mine has gum under it, too, and it's probably been there ever since I was a minimum wager.

Yes, I used to work at this shop—called Shake, Shake, Shake—in the touristy Colorado hamlet of Longdale. That was somewhere around the time when Lady Gaga wore a dress made of meat, and I fantasized about Justin Beiber singing "Baby" to me while I drifted off to sleep.

I've since moved up in the world. I'm no longer burning my fingers on the fry baskets or scraping melty ice cream from the blenders. Instead, as librarian, I scrape sticky cracker drool off toddler books and make sure the romance section of the mobile library in our town stays well stocked with the latest and greatest. Those pocket novels are full of dashing men way more exciting than anyone here in Longdale.

Speaking of dashing men, the one I'm supposed to meet here is over an hour late. Every minute I've been sitting here, he's become less dashing and more maddening. How dare he? I know he's gotten too big for his britches for our silly game, but geez, he could have let me know.

Should I send him hate texts? Or should I count myself lucky that we can finally forget this charade and move on with our lives?

I take in the shop, with its neon words of "Shake, Shake, Shake" at an angle in the window. The whole aesthetic is *Saved by the Bell* meets Beachy Shabby Chic. Longs Peak and the Flatirons loom in the distance, a rugged and wild panoramic.

Casting ornery thoughts about Oliver, I consider leaving the shake shop and going home. He's not here yet, but I always have the niggling fear that my grandparents might see us together, which would cause a lot of hand wringing and forehead wrinkling. Even though I'm a grown woman, have a Master's Degree in library science, and live on my own, I still worry about that. They *hate* the Tates.

The shake shop isn't exactly my grandparents' scene, and they haven't told me they're coming into town, but you never know. A small part of me likes that the fear makes it even more exciting.

Look at little Sophie now, living dangerously.

I might as well tattoo a sleeve of pythons on my arm and quit flossing my teeth.

I twiddle my thumbs and look up and down the street. Chilled, I pull my jacket tighter around me. Why is Longdale windy and chilly tonight? It's

August, for heaven's sake. But it is August in the mountains of Colorado, so any range of temperatures is up for grabs.

I pull my book out of my bag, a Margaret Atwood novel, fitting for the melancholy that has settled in my bones. My thoughts meander around the words on the page, flicking to reflections of Oliver, the mobile library I run, and my petition for a new library location that I don't have to drive around and that doesn't smell like diesel.

The sky has grown dark, and the crowds from earlier have thinned. Trying my best to ignore the kid in the shop who's making it very clear he's ready to lock up any time now and *why are you sitting there all by yourself like a loner*, I unlock my phone for the twentieth time. Still no text from Oliver.

He's never been this late before.

When I first started working here at age sixteen, I heard a rumor that one of the Tate boys would be hired on. I'd hoped it would be the oldest, Sebastian. He was a senior at a high school in Denver and quite possibly the most gorgeous man to ever walk the halls of any high school in the state, maybe even the whole Intermountain West. He and his five brothers used to come to Longdale to live with their aunt every summer while their parents were off, jet-setting around the world, donating to charities and fancy stuff like that.

Instead, it was Oliver who showed up to work, and I'll admit, I was disappointed at first. Sebastian was mysterious and broody. Oliver's the goofy one. Still attractive in his own right, he had a reputation of being a comedic, non-committal flirt.

I didn't need that in my life. I needed a Gilbert Blythe. A Mr. Darcy. A *Jane Eyre*-esque Mr. Rochester.

But it didn't take long for me to forget all about the illusion of Sebastian and fall—hard—for Oliver.

We've only ever been friends, though. Solidly, resolutely *friends*.

The idea for our annual not-a-date thing came during our last shift here, right before we parted ways to go to separate colleges. I was feeling nostalgic, and as usual, Oliver picked up on it.

"Promise you'll meet me here every year until the day we die?" He'd asked, and his grin made my stomach flutter.

I tried not to pretend he was saying "the *day* we die" as in *we're going to go all* The Notebook *here and die on the same day because we're soul mates and can't live without each other.*

I thought for a moment before replying, "Only if you're buying. As a librarian, I won't exactly be rolling in the dough."

"Okay, I'll buy. You just have to show up."

"Fine," I said. "Sounds good. But what's going to happen when you're climbing an Icelandic mountain, or swimming with dolphins in the Caribbean? You're going to forget."

"Forget? Never." He glanced at my mouth, and my mind started playing games with me. I imagined that he wanted to kiss me. But it was an impossibility. We were friends and only friends.

The wind picks up again. I finish the chapter, search the street and parking lot, and twiddle again.

Finally, a text from Oliver: *I'm sorry, Sophie. Something came up. I can't come.*

Me: *Is everything okay?*

Oliver: *Yes. I'll explain later.*

A dull thud starts behind my eyes. My stomach burns.

He's not coming.

I scoot my chair back so I can rest my head in my palms. I always figured this day would come, that our annual meet-up would end. But that doesn't mean I have to be happy about it.

The only thing left to do now is go home and cuddle with Wilford, my Bernese Mountain Dog.

And you know what? I'll buy myself my own dang shake, thank you very much. I stand, and even with the denim jacket over my new, belted floral tank dress, the wind cuts through me.

I reach the counter and plop down my card. "Can I get a black licorice peanut butter cup shake, please?" I ask the kid. "Large."

He scowls in disbelief. "Really?" he asks.

My voice is calm, but there's a torrential sea boiling inside of me. "I know it's off the menu, but can you do it anyway?" Geez. He must be new or something.

I glance around the old walk-up building. A dash of disappointment and fear seasons my resolve. I take a big breath—I need to stop this game we have. I need to move on with my life.

Goodbye, Oliver Tate.

Chapter 2

Oliver

Eight Months Later

I press my foot harder on the gas pedal, waiting for my brother, Alec, to stop talking already and take a breath. Veins in his neck are popping out. His nervous energy has me speeding up, which is never a good idea in this town. I've been pulled over on Lakeside Road a few too many times.

We take the last bend before passing the "Welcome to Longdale, population 2,514" sign.

"Oliver," Alec says. "Everyone thinks the new quarterback, a twenty-one-year-old baby, fresh out of college is gonna turn the franchise around." He sighs and scowls—which is pretty typical for him ever since his NFL career-ending knee injury the year before. "They're delusional," he complains.

I better slow down because if I get clocked going the speed my S-class Mercedes was born to do, I'll get pulled over for sure. Or, at the very least, we'd get an online complaint on the Tate International Resorts' virtual comment card page from some of the residents here in town.

It wouldn't be the first time Longdalers complained about our personal lives on the internet. And their complaints had nothing to do with the softness of the towels or the thickness of the mattress toppers because we haven't even opened yet.

And just to be clear, the softness and thickness of Tate International's amenities are unmatched in the industry.

I slow even more as I approach the first stoplight inside city limits. I figure there are fewer than ten stoplights in the entire town. Sleepy couldn't even begin to describe Longdale, which was one reason the whole state of Colorado had been abuzz over us, the Tate family, building one of our five-star resorts here.

We arrive at Alec's destination, a small eatery where he's meeting with a couple of former teammates from the San Antonio Wolves. I'm glad they came into town, even for just a quick trip. Alec's been bored and grumpy since he had to quit football.

"Thanks, man," he says. He flashes me an apologetic look. He doesn't exactly have a driver's license right now. Let's just say he had a rough time after his injury last fall.

"It's not a prob—" I stop short and sit up in my seat.

Is that who I think it is? Several yards in front of us, across the eatery parking lot and past an empty patch of weeds, I see a woman crouching on the pavement. She's hiding behind the mobile library, a brightly painted, old school bus. She's wearing a skirt that doesn't come close to covering her knees and she looks a whole lot like Sophie Lawson, one of my few friends in Longdale.

She used to be one of my best friends. After I didn't make it to our standing, annual thing…it's not a date…I'm not sure she'd still call me that.

I grunt out a laugh and chew my mint gum harder as the scene unfolds before me. It's Sophie, alright. I know Alec is still talking, but I'm hearing nothing, because…it's Sophie.

Her head peers around the corner of the bus before zipping back around, like she doesn't want to be seen. She puffs out a quick, short breath to try to move the hair out of her face, her right hand steadying herself against the back of the mobile library as her left hand tries, unsuccessfully, to tug her tight, black skirt down.

The skirt doesn't budge at all.

Alec finally stops talking and shakes my shoulder. "Oliver."

I should just unlock the door so he can get out and I can drive back to the resort. But if I move, I might miss something.

I see her in profile, her eyes squeezing shut. I know that look. She's focusing on her breathing. She did that a lot when the shake machine at Shake, Shake, Shake would blow a fuse.

"What in heaven's name are you up to, Sophie Wophie?" I muse under my breath. "Who are you hiding from?"

"Is that Sophie Lawson? The librarian?" Alec asks, leaning forward and squinting through the windshield.

Her head whips around frantically, as if looking for an escape route. I sink down low so she won't see me. Why I feel the need to hide is confusing. I should just wave or drive over there and say "hi."

But I don't want to make myself known quite yet. She's hiding from something or someone. And besides, it's fun watching her. I've always liked watching her. Not in an inappropriate or stalker way, of course. We've never been more than friends.

I stop myself from rolling my window down and calling her name. I don't want to give her away. I've witnessed many pickles Sophie got herself into back in the day and this seems no different.

Where is a big tub of obscenely buttered popcorn when I need it? This is the most entertaining thing I've seen since I arrived in town a couple of weeks ago.

She frowns, then picks a piece of lint off that skirt that is dangerously sexy...do I dare use that word to describe Sophie? If she knew I was thinking that, she'd punch me in the arm.

Continuing to crouch, she shifts her weight to her other side. Her hammies must be screaming. I know mine would be if I were crouching like that. The circulation would be cut off. The dark-haired beauty could lose a limb if she isn't careful.

She is beautiful. She always has been. But that doesn't mean I can do anything about it. I'm not settling down. Not at least until I'm retired from my job. Sophie wants a husband and family—a point we've argued over for years. I'll let my five brothers buy cute houses in Suburbia and shop at Costco every weekend with their wives and gaggles of kids. I've got other things to do.

Not that any of that has happened for us Tate brothers—yet. Alec has had enough heartache for one lifetime, so he's good with being single. And Henry was married briefly. All he has to show for it is an amazing daughter he rarely gets to see and scars from a messy divorce.

No, thank you.

"You should go over and say hi," Alec says. "She's the only friend you've got around here."

"I don't need friends. I have brothers," I say. It's a version of what mom says. That no one would have our back like our brothers. She's always trying to coax us to get along.

Maybe I should turn the car off and get out? Maybe I should holler her name?

I chuckle again as she peers around the side of the mobile library and quickly straightens back to hiding. I can see her face, in profile, scrunched up with worry. She sticks a pinkie finger in between her teeth. She still bites her nails?

Sophie, Sophie, Sophie.

"Is that the county mobile library?" Alec asks. "It's—seen better days."

"According to Sophie, the bus's name is Scott." I laugh, remembering that conversation about F. Scott Fitzgerald, or some such author. "When she graduated with her Master's, she found it in the back of the school district bus barn and renovated it. Without officially being hired on by the county yet. She had to write online articles and waitress to fund it and keep her own lights on."

Alec wrinkles his brow and nods. "She must really like books."

"She thinks it's her personal mission to get people reading. Longdale hadn't had a library for years at that point, and that wasn't acceptable to her." I smile when I remember her raging over the fact that the city librarian had retired to Arizona and Longdale hadn't replaced her.

He points up the street. "I remember something about the old building on the corner being condemned?"

I nod. "Black mold. It was a mess."

Alec points to the bus Sophie is crouching behind. "So's that."

"You should have seen it before she did her magic. Trust me, this is an improvement. She's been driving it around for ten years now. And the inside's actually pretty nice."

Not that I've seen it in a long while.

She's back on her hands and knees, crawling on the pavement. I cringe, worried about her skinning her knees. Maybe she's in some kind of trouble and needs help. Except she doesn't like being saved. Or helped. She's like a three-year-old learning to put her shoes on. She told the manager of the shake shop, "I can do it myself!" multiple times.

Wow, that brings up memories of a former life.

Well, former life for me. From the looks of it, Sophie's still up to her old shenanigans here in Longdale. She'll never leave, not for any extended amount of time. There are two things I'm sure of when it comes to Sophie: she loves black licorice peanut butter cup shakes—size large—and she loves Longdale.

Alec claps my shoulder. "Well, you have fun. Thanks for the ride." He leans forward to block my line of vision. "And if you don't go over there and say hi, it's just going to keep getting more and more awkward between you two." He opens the car door and starts to climb out. "You can't afford not to make things right again. She puts up with you, doesn't she?"

Since I got here a couple of weeks ago, I've been hanging out with Alec most evenings. We watch sports on TV at either my place or his. He's been staying in the small two-story house that was included in the sale of the property the resort now sits on. He's claimed it as his own, which is fine, as long as he doesn't become too much of a hermit as he frets and stews about his professional football career being over.

I made the mistake of telling him about how I'd missed last year's closing night. I had to tell him since he was calling me a loser for hanging out at home. I couldn't even bring myself to hang out with Alec because the guy has a gnarly chip on his shoulder. He's been antisocial since losing his college girlfriend way before he tore up his knee.

Sophie doesn't seem to hear me close the driver's side door and walk across the gravel. As I step in the small, empty lot towards her, I see she hasn't changed in a year and a half. The thick, brown curls still go halfway down her back. Today she has a bunch of curls tied away from her face with one of those velvety elastic things. And there's a piece of her hair that keeps falling over her eyes.

The memories start creeping up, and my heartrate does, too. Thoughts of closing up the shop with her filter through my mind, mixing with newer memories of our yearly meet-up and texting each other almost every day.

By the time I step out of the empty lot and back on concrete, she's got her whole body turned away from me. She doesn't see me yet. I'll just crouch down beside her and—

"Ah!" She startles and wobbles off balance. "Gaaahhh," she moans, grabbing my shirt as she starts to topple over. I only manage to slow the fall. She lands on her hip with an "oof," and I lurch forward, doing my best not to crush her beneath me.

Her mouth hangs open before cognition registers on her face. She scowls, her eyes narrowing. "Oliver?" It comes out as a whisper with some bite to it.

I go back to crouching, my head trying to move on from thoughts of how I'd accidentally pinned her on the ground. "How are you?" I whisper as I extend a hand to help her back into her recognizance stance.

She looks at my hand, ignores it, and then her features rearrange into a more pleasant expression. "I'm peachy. And you?"

I bounce my open palm up and down a couple of times. "Do you need some help?"

"No," she says. "My legs are—I just need a minute."

I glance down at the pavement, hoping she's not getting too much dirt on that amazing skirt of hers. Plus, her knees are red. She glances up to the closed window above us.

My legs are already cramping and so I sit cross-legged next to her.

"What are you doing here?" she whispers. Her gaze rakes over me, her expression unreadable.

"I was dropping Alec off at a lunch thing and happened to see you, um, behind the mobile library." I can't stop my grin from spreading. "Are you sure you're alright?"

She hisses out a shush and gets up into a high kneeling position, leaning closer to the bus, her ear to the metal.

Her eyes move around rapidly, and then she slumps down. "Like I said, I'm peachy. But I'm really trying to stay out of someone's way here, so if you don't mind going back to whatever it is you were doing before, that'd be great."

Her tone is happy-go-lucky, but her face betrays a certain chill. She reaches out a hand. "Catch up later, though?" she asks.

"Do you need me to go bust someone up for you? Did the board find out it was you who toilet papered the school before graduation?" I hadn't lived in Longdale during the school years, just the summers. But Sophie had told me all about her unusual display of rebellion.

She's not laughing at my little joke, and I realize my earlier fears weren't unfounded. She's mad at me.

Her voice goes even softer as she frowns. "I'm waiting back here until someone leaves, that's all. I'm not in the mood to talk to him." Her gaze flicks again to the window above us.

A surge of protectiveness overcomes me. "I'll go tell him to leave you alone. If he can't take the hint that you're not interested..."

"Oliver." She rolls her eyes. "Please. It's not like that. It's...sort of a business matter that I really don't want to do, so if you could please just—"

I jerk my head in the direction of my car. "Well, let's go then. I'll drive you around until he leaves."

She looks over at my car. "That's yours?" She rolls her eyes again. "Figures."

What? I like cars, and I can afford it.

But I don't say any of that. Instead, I stand and pull my keys out of my pocket. "Do you want a ride or not?"

She shoots me a look of death. "There's a window just above your head." Her whisper is harsh. "He's in there talking to Violet, who is stalling for me, hopefully. So I can't just go walking over to your car. He'll see me." She gazes at me, and I'm back in high school again, thinking her brown eyes have the most incredible glints of gold but knowing that if I were to say something like that to her, she might not respond well. Would she get mad? Would she ask what's wrong with me? Would she pretend I never said it?

It's that unknown that has settled Sophie into the "nothing more than a friend" zone. That and our completely opposite life goals.

"Who's Violet?" I ask. "Is she in on this secret plot?"

"On paper, she's my part-time assistant, but in reality, she's my steady, way more organized right-hand man—er, woman. She just got back from a cross-country tour of a bunch of independent bookstores."

"Huh, she sounds great." I glance up at the window and can't see what's going on through the glass. "I've got you," I whisper, placing my finger on my lips and beginning to walk backwards. "And besides, even if you stood up to your full height, he still wouldn't see you." I gesture with my hand to indicate her short stature.

Before she can get after me for teasing her, I spin around and stride back to my car. I'd sort of forgotten how Sophie makes everything fun, but it's unintentional. Like she's trying to tell the whole world that she's all good, but the world just keeps pointing out to her that nothing about her is normal at all. She needs to stop trying to convince it she is.

And sidenote: she's "not normal" in the best way possible. Really. It's the best compliment I could give anyone.

I find myself smiling as I get in my car and back up, and my grin gets even bigger as I drive out onto the street and turn in to where the mobile library sits—the city and county offices parking lot. I zoom around it to pick her up.

She steps towards the car and casts one last glance behind her before throwing the passenger door open and sliding inside.

It's not until I'm pulling out of the parking lot that I look in the rearview mirror and notice an older guy clanging down the metal ramp of the mobile library. He's got a look of confusion and anger, so I speed up, the tires squealing as I peel out on Main.

Speeding tickets and disapproving online comments be darned. I'm on a quest for Sophie. And nothing's going to stop me from helping her.

Chapter 3

Sophie

Oliver's car is *nice.* I feel like my bargain skirt is defiling it just by sitting in it. Especially since my skirt probably has tar dust from the blacktop I so gracefully fell on earlier.

His car is the kind with tan leather everything. I knew he loved cars and spent incredible amounts of money on them. I'd never been inside one, though. He always flies in for our standing not-a-date every August. But now, according to the grapevine, he's here to stay for awhile.

I have to focus on the car again, because I'm trying not to stare at him. He's a vision. A toned, dark-haired, brown-eyed vision in his untucked, lavender oxford shirt, slim tan pants cut above the ankle, and off-white suede derby shoes.

This day is not turning out like I thought it would. First, I had to hide from Mr. Wallis behind the mobile library I've affectionately named Scott.

And now I'm in a car with Oliver and my feelings are ping ponging around, giving me a headache.

Or, I might have a headache because Oliver is taking the turns on the empty road at an irresponsible speed. I start to worry about the cop situation, but I really shouldn't. We have a county police force, and the station's ten miles away. At any given moment, you've got a good chance that the two patrol cars are in a different town from the one you're in, something that people in the know take advantage of.

Thoughts of what I could and should say to Oliver unsettle me. But one thing is sure: I'm not going to bring up the fact that he missed our last scheduled closing day thingamajig what-have-you. I'm pretending like it didn't happen—that it was a non-issue.

"Why is the big bus named Scott again?" Oliver asks.

"Scott's a very literary name. It's perfect for him. Orson Scott Card, F. Scott Fitzgerald, Walter Scott, Scott O'Dell...need I go on?"

"I get it now," he says with a chuckle.

His pause pricks my curiosity. I know he's about to dive into something serious.

"Soph, I wanted to apologize about last August." Oliver glances at me before training his gaze back on the road.

Well, that was fast.

His words hang in the air, and I'm suddenly uncomfortable. I can't let on that I was bothered by his ditching me.

Of course, I was sad he didn't come. It hurt. And I promised myself that I'd never let Oliver Tate hurt me. I can't care enough to have it hurt.

For the most part, that promise to myself has worked out fine.

I change the subject. "Thank you for saving my bacon back there. Seriously. The dude would not leave."

It's his turn to change the subject. "Two things."

There's a hitch in my breath. That thing he does, where he says, "two things" is an Oliver thing. He's been doing it since he was sixteen years old, and I find it adorable. It usually means something funny and ridiculous. But this time, I'm wrong, because he goes all serious on me, like he's about to recite Tolstoy's *War and Peace*.

"One, who are we running from? And two, about closing night—"

I can't talk about it because then he'll think I care, and I don't. So, I go for the slightly lesser of two evils.

"I don't know exactly why he wants to talk to me, but I strongly suspect it has something to do with Longdale Days, as in he's going to ask me to run it." I shunt out a breath. "I can't. I won't do it."

"Wow. Run Longdale Days? Like, be in charge of the whole thing? That's huge, Soph."

My stomach tingles. He called me Soph. Not many people do that anymore. I should tell him not to.

"You're saying it like it's a good thing."

He uses his blinker to turn left and I'm glad to know he hasn't abandoned all safe driving practices.

"I'm impressed," he says. "You get to wear a hat and ride a classic car in the parade."

"No, because I'm not going to say yes." Although the thought of having everyone see me as chairperson of Longdale Days gives me a brief flash of triumph. Like, *Look at little Sophie Lawson now, ya geeks!*

I continue. "I've been saying yes for years to everything the county council has been asking me to do because I'm petitioning for a new, brick and mortar location for the library. So there's been this *quid pro quo* idea out there—I'll scratch your back if you scratch mine. I'll volunteer, I'll head committees, I'll do whatever they need so they'll support the petition. But this?" I shake my head. "It's too much. I'm not going to do it."

Oliver gives a hearty nod. "Good. If people have been taking advantage of your skills and not giving you the support you need, then I'm one hundred percent in favor of you not doing it." He steals another glance at me. "But why didn't you just tell the guy that? What's his name again?"

I never said his name. It's complicated and messy and I especially don't want Oliver to know about any of that.

"He's just on the county council." I wave it away. "And I'm going to tell him no. I've already told Sue Leavitt I'm not interested, and she was supposed to tell the council. I don't know why he'd track me down at the mobile library."

I give a little laugh, and I'm pretty sure Oliver knows it's laced with nerves. Because I totally know why that man showed up today, and I can't bring myself to talk about it.

"My offer still stands. I'll talk to him for you. Tell him to leave you alone and that you're not going to be chairing anything, especially Longdale Days." His brow scrunches down. "Isn't that coming up in like a month, anyway?"

I nod. "Five weeks. Yes. And Sue Leavitt stepped down. She's been in charge of it for as long as I can remember, but she had back surgery and said that was her ticket out." I shake my head. "And her eyes sparkled like she was thinking, 'Finally, my pretty.'" I bring my hands together to rub them sneakily. "Someone to unwittingly take over the worst, most thankless job in the county.'"

Oliver laughs. I've missed the way I can make him laugh. And I wasn't going to. I knew he was back in town, so I've been practicing putting up my wall. The wall that helped me survive every summer in high school with him.

Because the truth is, he's a Tate boy. And for reasons I can't begin to understand, there's just something about them Tate boys.

Well, I *can* understand it because they're all handsome and exciting. All six of them. And though they always had plenty of money, it's been within the last ten years that the oldest, Sebastian, who is two years older than Oliver and me, struck it rich in the resort industry.

Important sidenote: I have not crushed on all six Tate men. I'm not that kind of woman. I only ever had feelings for three of them, okay? And it's three too many.

Also important to note? I have cared for other men besides the Tates.

"You keep avoiding the subject," Oliver says.

"What subject?"

He pauses and sighs. "When I didn't come last year. I'm sorry about that."

I give my robotic giggle again. "Do you think I'm upset with you or something? Oliver, no. It's nothing. I'd basically forgotten too, until that night and I was like, 'oh yeah, it's the Oliver thing.'"

I rotate my body to better face him. The more I talk, the more I'm convincing myself. "So really, it's no big deal. It's way past time we stopped that. I mean, someday, maybe even soon, we'll marry and have kids and it wouldn't be practical to meet up for a milkshake from Shake, Shake, Shake."

I laugh, hopefully more convincingly this time. And I will myself to discard the thought that when I said "we'll marry and have kids," an image of Oliver and I having a family together pressed on my brain.

He lets out a long breath. "Good. I'm glad you aren't upset about that. I've been feeling bad, you know? And especially about not letting you know beforehand or following up."

Yep. That's the real kicker for me. That's what hurt the most. He owes me an explanation.

"Oliver! I told you, it's no big deal," I lie. "Besides, I should thank you because when you didn't show up, I actually…" I make a fist and chew on my thumb. "I met someone."

His brows shoot up, sky high. "Really? Who?"

"No." I stare at him and point a finger in the air. "It's your turn to spill. What have you been up to?"

He shakes his head and licks his lips, a frustrated tone coursing through him. "Fine. Tight-lipped. I get it. Anyway, Soph, I *am* sorry. Something came up. It was sort of a private family thing. And by the time things were taken care of, I don't know…I didn't know how to bring it up."

"So you texted me some pictures of your food the next day." I nod, but I'm wondering about his family emergency. I hope everyone's okay.

"Yeah, I guess I did. That was a jerk move."

"Will you stop? I've told you it's okay. It's time we quit that, anyway."

The car starts to slow, and he doesn't answer. Instead, he whips his head around. "Do you think it's safe to pull over now? We could walk around the park."

"I should probably get back to Scott. I'm sure Violet's wondering where I went." I want to walk around the park with him, but I just can't. And having to get back to my job is only one of the many reasons.

"But if the guy's still there…I say we wait. Better safe than sorry."

I nod. "True. One time around the park."

We get out of his car into May's brilliant sun and quickly fall into the same stride as we traipse in the grass, which has grown long with all the rain we had the month before.

I tell him the story of when a couple got engaged outside of Scott last month after having an epic argument that I heard only bits and pieces of. He tosses his head back in a laugh, and I'm reminded of how much I like having that effect on him.

I see a car parked next to his as we round the corner. The park is small. It's Longdale—of course it's small. We've nearly reached it when someone gets out of the car, and I gasp. "No!" I stop abruptly.

Oliver gives me a questioning look before trailing my gaze. "He followed us here? How? I'm usually so good at losing a tail. Henry's taught me a thing or two."

Henry is his brother. And, fine, I'll admit he's one of the Tate boys I used to have feelings for, for like ten seconds. He's all quiet and mysterious and people gossip about him possibly being a government spy.

We slow our steps as we approach the last man I wanted to see. Well, almost the last man I wanted to see.

Oliver leans in. "You've got this, Soph. It's best to tell him no now and get it over with." He practically whispers it in my ear, and my shoulder and upper arm break out in goosebumps at the feel of his breath on my skin. "Just give me a signal and I'll step in if you need back up, okay?"

I say okay and my throat dries up. I've disliked this man ever since I met him months ago, but I'm unprepared for the rush of disdain that comes up when I see him leaning against his car, his arms crossed over his chest.

"Sophie, I tried to track you down at the library," Mr. Wallis says, scratching his stubbly chin.

"I was out back—sweeping."

Sorry to the honesty gods. I'll make a burnt sacrifice to you later.

Mr. Wallis moves away from his car and glances at Oliver before looking back at me. "I'm glad I caught you. I've been trying to call and email you. And my secretary emailed you, too."

"Right. I meant to get in touch with you. It's been so busy at work." *Sorry again to the honesty gods.*

Mr. Wallis clearly doesn't believe that. "Well, this needs to be pinned down. There's a lot to do." He grins widely. "And I think you'll be honored to know that the council decided, overwhelmingly, to give you the opportunity to be our chairperson for Longdale Days this year." He unlocks his phone, and types. "I can send you the agenda, but the calendar's mostly filled out and decided on. You'll just put it on the city's tab at the grocery store and whatnot, so you wouldn't have to pay for anything out of pocket."

Oliver slides his arm around me, his hand resting on my shoulder. Mr. Wallis looks up from his phone and reddens, but continues speaking to me. "I was telling Troy it's time to have you two over for dinner again. Longdale Days isn't the only thing that needs to get planned out." He beams. "We've got a wedding to plan, too."

Oliver's grip tightens on my upper arm.

Wedding? Oh no. No no no.

"Mr. Wallis, there's been a mistake. I never agreed to chair Longdale Days. You'll need to find someone else." Even though my heart is whacking against my ribcage, my voice is strong and clear.

"But Troy said you'd love to do it. And everyone thinks you'd do a great job. Now, it's decided. I'll send you the calendar and some old mockups for advertising, although if you want to create brand new ones, be my guest."

My jaw aches from clenching it. This guy is impossible. "No. I can't do it. I'm sorry."

He says nothing, just stares at Oliver's hand on my shoulder. Finally, he scratches the back of his head. "I don't know what makes you think this is something you can just turn down. We need you, Sophie. And there's the library petition to think of." His voice isn't cheerful anymore.

Yeah. That's the risk of my refusal—getting on the council's bad side and potentially harming any chances for a new library.

Oliver widens his stance. "And I don't know why you're not listening to Ms. Lawson. She said no and that's final." Oliver's lips press together so hard the area above them goes white. "Besides, she couldn't do it even if she wanted to." He moves his hand to my elbow. "Because I've hired her to get some things ready for the resort's grand opening in a month and she won't have any spare time to do Longdale Days."

I glance at him. Hired me?

Mr. Wallis stammers, his gaze on me hardening. "I can't believe my son's marrying you."

I don't know who looks more surprised. My almost former future father-in-law. Or Oliver.

Chapter 4

Oliver

Uh. Come again?

I look at Sophie in profile. Then I look at the jerk who is not only verbally abusive to her but has said something about Sophie marrying his son.

I look at Sophie again. She's engaged? My hand now feels stiff against the silky fabric of her blouse. I should remove it because apparently I'm touching someone else's fiancée. And my hand has just started sweating. I should drop it, but for some reason, I can't.

Just one more thing I need to apologize to Sophie for.

Soph, sorry for sweating on this nice shirt of yours. Also, sorry for breaking a promise to you last year. Oh, and also? Sorry for the way my thoughts are freaking out about this new development.

Sophie's engaged. She's going to marry someone else. I steal a glance at her left hand. No ring. She doesn't seem like the type who would forgo wearing an engagement ring because she likes jewelry.

And apparently she likes some dude enough to marry him.

Sophie's eyes are dark, and she worries her lip. Finally, she speaks up. "You need to have a conversation with Troy, Mr. Wallis."

She clears her throat and gives me a side glance. I don't know how to read it. I used to be good at understanding all her expressions.

Why didn't she tell me she's engaged? How did I not know she was dating—in love with someone? We text almost every day, although the texts have slowed down some since I missed closing night.

At her glance, I drop my hand from her arm. No sweat stain from the faucet-like pores of my palm, thank goodness. But a strange whisper of betrayal pulses through my veins. Not because she's involved with someone else, but because she didn't tell me.

"Oliver Tate is right." Her head points in my direction. "I'm too busy helping them prepare for the grand opening to take care of Longdale Days."

It's weird the way she emphasizes "Tate." Like she's wielding a dirty word.

The man's hardened gaze goes from Sophie to me, his eyes boring into mine. I can see how he won his position on the county council.

"You're one of the Tates, huh?" he asks.

"Yes, I am." I pause. "And we're in dire need of Ms. Lawson's many talents, so good luck finding someone to chair Longdale Days." I force a grin. "I'll have our PR rep get ahold of you about Tate International becoming a sponsor. We'd love to contribute."

Mr. Wallis's face goes from anger, to confusion, to something like be-grudged gratitude. He's Sophie's future father-in-law. My stomach drops. What's going on with me? It's not like I ever thought she and I would get married. I almost chuckle at the thought. Sophie's the marrying kind, but I'll let her have that life choice. Life is too short for me to do something like that. What good is having five brothers, if not for the security that at least a couple of them will marry and continue the Tate line?

"Sophie, I'll talk to Troy." His face is splotchy. "You don't have to decide yet."

Everything in her tightens up—her smile is soaked in antiseptic. He leaves and the air in the park feels strained, like there's not enough oxygen. The altitude at Longdale never bothered me before.

But Sophie's never been engaged before.

As I turn to her, she won't meet my gaze. That's when a slice of panic gets my heart racing. And then I'm disgusted with myself. What right do I have to be upset about Sophie getting married? We've never dated. We've never been on one single date. Those August meet-ups? Totally platonic.

There were women. And I've dated my fair share. But then there's Sophie. On a level by herself.

A jolt zips through me.

"Um, congratulations, Sophie." With the blood rushing through my ears, I can't tell exactly how pathetic I might sound.

Sophie's gaze moves rapidly over me, her brow jammed down. "Oliver. I'm not engaged."

"What?"

"I was never officially engaged, okay?" She tugs her hand through her dark curls. "Troy blew things out of proportion and his family thought we were more serious than we were." She finishes with an, "Ugh!"

I hate myself for the wave of relief that's making its way through me. "Still. I didn't even know there was a Troy to begin with." Why am I so upset by this?

"I told you I met someone." She resumes our walk, her steps dull.

"Well, 'met someone' could mean anything." My face is starting to fill with blood once more. "I'm confused as to how his family could assume you're getting married when you weren't? What's the deal with that?"

"It's really complicated." Her cheeks flush and she shakes her head. "I didn't tell you because I didn't know if you'd care. And you never mention the women you date." She interrupts my protest before I can even start. "I know you date, Oliver. But we never talk about it. Besides, things with Troy happened so fast."

Things with Troy. Why do I hate that phrase so much? And she is right. We set an unspoken precedence a long time ago. We don't talk about our romantic lives. Wasn't hard. I've never had a serious relationship to speak of. And I'd assumed Sophie hadn't either.

We always talked about our work, families, and when something embarrassing happened. She was the first person I contacted when I lost my wallet in Brisbane and when I broke my hand in Beijing. I got a late night call from her when her sister had to have emergency surgery.

But the love stuff? Nope. Nothing.

"Look, we were never officially engaged," she says. "I never had a ring. And he and I aren't right for each other." She whirls to me and holds up a hand. "I don't have to defend my engagement, or lack thereof, to you, Oliver."

She scowls and her words have bite. I'm shuffling through reasons why she could be upset. Maybe it's still because of what happened last August but somehow it feels bigger than that.

"I know," I insist.

"We don't talk about stuff like this. For all I know, *you* could be engaged."

"Well, I'm not. You know I'm reserving that honor for my brothers."

She lifts a shoulder like she doesn't care. But her eyes hold a different story. "Why can't you get married?" Her hands fly up into the air and then slap her thighs on the way down. "That whole, 'my brothers can carry on the Tate name' thing is just so dumb." She bends her knees as she raises her arms again. "You can all get married. It's not like there's a moratorium on the number of Tate boys who are allowed to walk down the aisle."

"Why the hostility? You've always known I'm not interested in marriage."

"You're only thirty-three years old, Oliver. You haven't wanted to get married yet, but that doesn't mean you won't change your mind."

"And why does this matter right now? We're talking about you," I shoot back.

Her gaze softens, her brown and gold eyes brimming with tears. "I just want to understand, that's all."

I sigh and begin walking again. "I decided when I was young that if marriage meant you argued a lot and left your kids for months at a time, then I wouldn't do it. Why would I want that? Besides, having a family with the job I have? I couldn't drag them along while I'm scouting locations for Sebastian."

I glance at her quickly, and her expression seems calm. But expressions can be deceiving. We walk in silence.

Finally, I can't take the quiet anymore. "I don't know what to say. Do I say I'm sorry that things didn't work out with him? Because something about this seems a little off. I'm glad you're not getting married to this Troy guy because I think I know you well enough to know if you're in love, and this is feeling like…that's not the case." I bring my still-a-little-sweaty hand up to massage the back of my neck.

"Well, don't you just know everything?" She's snarky…seething. "I was nearly engaged to the guy. Of course I had feelings for him."

I'm glad she's using the past tense, but this conversation is way out of my league. Clearly, my emotions can't be trusted right now.

"I'm sorry, Soph."

She's quiet—almost defeated. "You've said sorry like ten times today. There's nothing to be sorry about. I dated someone. Some people got the wrong idea about how much our relationship had progressed." Her voice grows sharp. "I'm in my thirties and I live in a small town that, when it's not peak tourist season, might have maybe less than ten eligible guys for me." She gives a humorless laugh and stops to face me again. "So, forgive me for entertaining the idea off and on. Troy isn't a bad guy."

Her eyes are fiery, and that twists me up inside. "Hey," I say softly. "Talk to me. Tell me all about it or…nothing about it, whatever you want."

She looks so sad that I pull her into a hug without a second thought. We had the standard greeting and saying goodbye hugs every year. But this one feels different.

Slow your row, Oliver.

Just because Sophie is soft and vulnerable, doesn't mean I need to get caught up in this hug.

She shudders in my arms, sniffing twice before pulling away. "It's fine. Truly." She swipes a finger under her left eye and glances at it, probably to see if she's smudged her makeup.

"Well, that's too bad that people think you're engaged. You should get a robocall going in town to let everyone know you aren't and never were."

"That's not a bad idea, since, you know, Longdale gossip." She shakes her head. "I think people were just happy for me that I'd found someone."

"What was so wrong with him?" I'm curious. I've never quite figured out what kind of guy Sophie likes. Except for my brother, Sebastian. I know she used to like him. I fight the urge to scratch a deep itch, one that comes over me every time I think of Sophie crushing on Sebastian way back when.

"I kept asking myself that," she says. "Because, on paper, he was great. He has a good job in IT. He's kind to his mother and sisters. He didn't mind that I liked to read on our dates sometimes."

"Wait, wait, wait. He's an IT guy?" I know I'm pulling a face. But I can't help it. Just because IT guys save the world with their know-how doesn't mean they're good enough for Sophie.

She shoves my shoulder. "What's so wrong with that? He made good money." She sounds like she's trying to convince herself along with me.

I stifle a laugh. "I just never pictured you with an IT guy, that's all."

A smile plays about her lips. "You've imagined me with someone?"

No, she did not. I will not take that bait. "Well, when you were in love with Sebastian, I was so annoyed that I had to come up with alternatives for you in my mind, you know? The great, great grandson of Jack the Ripper would be better suited for you than Sebastian."

Her cheeks redden like they always do when I mention her long-ago feelings for my older brother. At least, I hope they're dead and gone.

"Wow. Thanks a lot for that." She fluffs the back of her dark curls. "You'd rather I marry the descendant of a slasher."

"No. I'm just proving a point here." We continue walking, our footsteps on the cement pathway in sync. "You can't marry an IT guy. You need someone more interesting." The park's playground is empty, but across the grass, there's a pick-up game of soccer amongst a group of teens.

She plays with a lock of her hair. "Good news, Oliver. I'm *not* marrying an IT guy."

"Whew. That's a relief." I exaggerate my comment, but she probably has no idea how relieved I really am. I don't have that right, but my insides begin to calm.

"So, what happened?" I press. "Why aren't you telling me anything?"

Sighing, she hugs her arms. "I don't know. The whole thing was strange. There wasn't anything wrong with him, there just wasn't any spark. I searched for a spark because...I wanted there to be one. And it's not like he was that into me, either. I mean, he would have picked going fishing over hanging out with me any day of the week. So that was kind of a turn off."

"Soph. You can't like a guy who smells like fish."

This earns a tiny smile. "I don't. For the millionth time. Things are over with Troy."

"Except his family doesn't know that. Does *he* know that?"

"Yes! Of course he knows that. When I broke up with him in Fort Collins about a month ago, he agreed it was for the best, told me he saw this coming and wished me well. We split an Uber home and I haven't spoken to him since."

"You split an Uber?" My head is vacillating between numbness and wanting to introduce the guy to both of my fists. "After breaking up?"

Sophie's eyes widen, like she can hardly believe it either, but is still kind of bugged that I'm calling this out. Because no man splits an Uber with Sophie. She's not that kind of girl. She deserves much more than Uber. But if you have to, at least pay for it yourself. Geesh, if I ever meet this jerk Troy...

She starts giggling and it feels like we're teens in the shake shop again. I can't help but join in. Finally she comes up for air. "The sad part was, it wasn't even that awkward! We'd literally just broken up and the ride home was pleasant. I tell you, my life is just odd, you know?"

"Yes. Yes, it is."

I know she needs to return to work, but I don't want to take her back yet. Even though I usually have a brother or two to hang out with at any given time, I've sort of felt lonely. More than I care to admit. Being around Sophie feels really good. And bonus: she's not engaged!

"So, how about it? Why not actually help us with the grand opening?" I ask.

"What do you mean? The only skill I have that you might possibly need is my proficiency around a vacuum."

"You are an excellent vacummer." It used to be the only housework she liked doing. "But no. I was thinking maybe you could help curate our resort library."

She wheels around, clutching my arm. We come to a halt. "You're doing it? There's a library at the resort? I've been trying to convince you ever since you built the first one."

"I finally listened to you and insisted we add it to the plans. Sebastian fought me on it until the designer agreed. They're really popular now."

"I told you! This is so exciting." Her golden-brown eyes brighten. She's standing so close to me that it does something to my head. "Did you know there are people out there who won't go to a resort if it doesn't have a good library? And that was one of the first things I thought when I heard you were going to put a resort here in town, that since Longdale isn't exactly full of tons of stuff to do, a library is the perfect draw."

"Are you sure people care about a resort's library?"

"Well, not a whole lot of people, obviously, but Oliver, if you make it amazing it will be something that people notice and enjoy. It adds to the whole package." She smirks. "Besides, I'm that kind of people. I never go to a resort if it doesn't have a library."

"You never go to a resort."

Her grin was heart stopping. Everything. Dangerous. "So what? *If* I did, I'd check to make sure there was a library there. Are you mocking my poverty?"

"Never," I say. "Which brings me to the next subject. We'll compensate you for your time, obviously."

Her brows go in the air and her response is saucy. "You better."

"You'll do it? You'll curate our library and help us get it set up?" I want her to agree to it, even while I know this can't possibly be a good thing in the long run.

Her face stills, the planes and curves more beautiful than I've ever remembered. Or realized. "I'll come by tomorrow." She squeezes my upper arm before turning away, and that's when I realize we've circled back around to my car again. She gets in and I stand there, watching her. She leaves the door open. "Are you going to drive me back or do I need to call an Uber?"

"I'm coming," I push back. I close the door for her. An inexplicable hatred for Troy who had captured her heart pulses through me as I stroll to the driver's side door. I mostly believe her when she says it's truly over. That he was all wrong for her is embedded within every little fact I know about him. Yet I'm angry with him that he was such a chump, and mad that she started falling for someone so beneath her.

Somehow, I feel responsible for that. She met him on closing night, the night she was supposed to be with me. So I guess I'm angry at myself, too.

We drive back to Scott in low-key silence, my mind hopped up on realizations I've never taken the time to consider. I pull up to the old school bus that she'd painted with a map of the world dotted with famous books in every genre.

I remember when she drew out the design for me on napkins at Shake, Shake, Shake a few years ago. I hadn't taken the time to follow up on it much after that. I should have asked her about it more often. I should have asked her to send me photos of how it turned out.

A burning of regret hits my chest. I've treated her no better than Troy—and that's the worst pill to swallow.

Chapter 5

Sophie

I don't know if it was a good idea to come. It feels sort of dangerous. Not the thrilling kind of dangerous, the I'm-going-to-lose-my-lunch dangerous.

I'm standing in front of Tate International's Longdale Lake Resort and it's the most magnificent thing to ever grace this area.

Besides the actual area itself, you know, the untouched nature and all.

And Oliver himself. But that's neither here nor there.

They outdid themselves with this one. The gossip around town is that this is the nicest and best resort the Tate brothers have ever done. They're dedicated to protecting and preserving the ecosystem of Longdale Lake. That's why it's tiered, with all its levels and colors fitting into the natural landscape's divots and curves along the mountain. The design also maximizes views of the lake.

Except I feel guilty for liking it so much. I feel guilty for even being here. Ever since it was announced three years ago, my grandparents haven't let a single visit go by without them mentioning how terrible it is—how the resort will bring in traffic and pollution.

I don't know why they care so much. As soon as my sister and I graduated high school, they moved out of Longdale and back to Boulder—back to the life they'd had before the death of their daughter turned everything upside down.

Actually, scratch that. I know exactly why they care. The Tate brothers had never mentioned anything about building here until my grandfather's power company decided they wanted to put wind turbines in that exact spot. The Tates were upset by that and the way it would affect the landscape—each wind turbine needs a five-hundred-foot radius clear of trees to function. You add enough of those to make a difference in Longdale citizens' power bills and there goes acres and acres of Blue Spruce.

So, yes. My grandparents and the Tates are sworn enemies now. The back and forth and public fighting was all around town.

Don't tell my grandparents this, but I've secretly been Team Tate ever since.

I smooth the front of my black swing dress with the peter pan collar and cuffs. I paired it with simple black, peek-a-boo toe pumps, globe earrings and a single gold bangle. A girl's gotta dress up because this is sort of like a job interview. It just happens to be with Oliver Tate, the man I cannot seem to get out of my head. Maybe working for the Tates will force me to be professional—force me to move on.

And a resort library *is* a big deal. I feel honored that he trusts me with it. I guess my master's in library science isn't such a big waste after all, like my grandparents thought it would be.

I take in a ragged breath. Okay, time to go in there and make this work. Time to take Oliver from would-be-in-my-wildest dreams boyfriend to what he actually is now: My boss. Sort of.

I head up the stone steps to the massive oak sliding doors. It has bubbled panes of glass and the hardware looks like it's been aged a few hundred years on an Italian castle.

Wow. A mix of neutrals and stainless steel, this thing is like a polished, European post-modern cabin in the woods.

I breeze through the doors and I'm Little Orphan Annie walking into Daddy Warbuck's mansion. There's a massive oak reception desk and two seating areas opposite one another, both with ornate fireplaces and landscape paintings. The place smells like fresh paint. It's a blend between rustic and opulent. Not sure how they pulled that off, but they did.

"Sophie! You made it."

It's Oliver. He's shut-the-front-door handsome, and my arms and legs break out in goosies as proof.

He's wearing a black and white, buffalo plaid dress shirt and pink chinos. His sleeves are rolled up to his elbows. It's high-end, business casual with an Oliver flair. Most distracting? His cedarwood, minty pear scent. I have no idea what it's called but I'd know it anywhere.

And now I'm regretting my decision to spray my day-three hair with my dog Wilford's dry shampoo. Bad choice, even if it is juicy peach scented. I should have just washed my dang hair. I'd run out of the human variety of dry shampoo. And yes, it felt wrong using a dog product on my hair, okay? Not my proudest moment.

But I'm here with Oliver. I should have taken better care of my hair hygiene needs. I rub the top of my part, hoping the white powder has fully dissolved.

He strides across the tile floors. They're slate intermingled with a marbly tile.

"This place is..." I shake my head, my gaze going all around the vaulted ceilings.

"It's nice," he says. "Not that I can take any credit for it. Most of the decisions were made before I came on board for this one." He places a hand at the small of my back and leads me around the corner to the elevators.

Reason 574 that it was the right thing to break up with Troy. His touch never made me shiver like Oliver's does. Which could be a problem in our current situation, so I make a mental note—albeit a disappointed one—to avoid his physical touch.

Sidenote? I still can't believe I met Troy the night Oliver didn't show up. Maybe I looked at him like some sort of replacement?

In any case, this is my chance to ensure our business arrangement stays businessy. Not shivery. Businessy.

"You weren't always on board for the Longdale location?" I ask, side-stepping so that his hand drops from my back. Talking about the resort should be a safe topic.

Something in his expression does a stutter step before he continues, his gaze down the hall and out the side door. "No. I'd actually originally told Sebastian he'd have to get the Longdale Lake property up and running without me. I was busy with other projects for the company."

My stomach plunges to my knees when I realize that he'd tried not to move back to Longdale. He wasn't jumping at the chance to be here—the place I'll never move from, as I promised my mom.

We step into the elevator, and I wall up, like those hamster balls that make it so you can't lose the little guy. You know, the clear plastic things? I use that visual to remind myself to keep my feelings protected, and to not let anything get to me.

It's not always the healthiest metaphor to use. But it matters with Oliver. It's the only way to survive.

"You boys sure do stay busy," I say. "You have, what, ten resorts now?"

"Yeah. And this year is our tenth anniversary in business." He whistles low. "I can't believe it."

"What was more pressing than this place? I'm sure it's important to you all, since you spent every summer here."

He nods as we leave the elevator on the fourth floor.

"It's true. It is. It's smaller than we've ever done. And we've never built one in a secluded location like this."

"But you had to come and save us from those no good, very bad wind turbines."

His face falls. He knows it was my grandparents' company that tried to get those installed. He knows their company has struggled ever since they lost the land bid to the Tates. The tips of his ears burn pink.

"You know how I feel," I say, giving his shoulder a light shove. "I've told you before." I'd told him I'd rather a resort than those ugly monstrosities.

I love my grandparents. They're not exactly fans of Longdale, though. They didn't want their daughter, Marie, to follow her new husband here. But she did, and my younger sister and I were born and raised here, even though our father was out the door and out of our lives before Claire was even born.

My mom passed away from a swift-moving brain tumor when I was nine. My grandparents were kind not to uproot us when we'd had our only known parent taken from us. But they never could quite curb the bitterness over having to change their lives for us. It hangs in the air around them like smog.

Oliver interrupts the thoughts that always cause a dash of pain. "Now that you're here and inside, what do you think? Are you still glad you're not standing in a wind turbine field?"

"Yes. It's breathtaking." I take in the vaulted ceiling and balcony.

"And it's small enough that we're not going to have hundreds of people coming and going, taxing the town's resources."

"How many guest rooms are there?"

"Just fifty. All suites."

Our footsteps echo along the cozy, matte hardwood. "How does it feel for you?" I ask. "I know you never thought you'd make Longdale your home, as much as Aunt Stella wanted you all to."

"I don't know. It's a little strange. I flew in from Capri."

Ah, yes. He loves Capri. Oliver and I are opposites…it's good for me to be reminded of that every so often.

"How are the Capri deals coming along?"

"Lots of strings to pull, but things are happening." His eyes light up.

"I'm sure it's lovely there." I refrain from saying: *I'm sure the women are lovely there, too.*

"We needed boots on the ground, someone to take care of all the red tape and bureaucracy to get permits."

I knew it had become his passion project. "Well then, what convinced you to move here?"

"It's—I haven't moved here exactly." His gaze is trained on the floor. "I'm just renting this place up the hill. It started last Christmas when we were all in Denver. Sebastian was being a real sweetheart to me, you know, buttering me up."

"You mean, he wasn't a big grump like usual?"

"He wasn't. We played basketball the night before I went back to Capri and he says, "You can go back. But come to Longdale in the spring. I need you to run the operations at the resort, Oliver. You're the best, Oliver. You know, just stating the facts.""

I laugh.

"And I said okay, but it was only temporary. I'd work to get things up and running, make sure we were staffed and had the logistics in place, and then I'd go to Capri. And keep scouting other places, too. I told him I'd work on the Capri project remotely. Hopefully when I get back, we'll have broken ground."

"So, being here is an <u>exception</u>?"

"Yes," he says. "I haven't helped much with operations in the past. But now that the resort's almost ready, we've been getting things in place."

"How long are you going to stay in Longdale?" I brace myself for his answer.

"Seven months total."

My stomach flip flops. His stay really is going to be temporary. That's a good thing, I remind myself. "A strange number. Why not just half a year or a year? Make it even."

"Because Sebastian said, 'The number of free throws I make in a row is the number of months you have to stay on at Longdale Lake.'"

"And he made seven in a row?"

"Yeah," he says. "I'm lucky it wasn't more."

My chest tightens at his words.

"He choked when you consider how he was good enough to play for the NBA back in his prime," Oliver says.

Sebastian had played some in college. I, personally, was totally lost when it came to sports. A puppy has more hand eye coordination than I do, and puppies don't even have hands.

But the Tate brothers? They were all athletic in one way or another. Alec used to play for the NFL until he blew out his knee last year.

"So, you'll only be here for seven months," I say.

"Yeah. I need to get back to scouting future locations." He glances at me, his forehead wrinkled.

There's something in his expression that's asking me what I think about that.

Why he cares is a mystery to me. I'm tempted to tell him to stop chasing the world and settle down already. I'm also tempted to say that I'm really glad he's here, and maybe he'll like it so much he won't want to leave.

But I don't. Remember the whole hamster ball thing?

Because I'm such an expert at expressing my feelings, I change the subject. "The view here is nice." I point to the wall of windows. A dense forest of pines and Blue Spruce is dotted with bursts of Quaking Aspen groves. I can practically smell the Christmas tree scent from here.

"You're right. It's incredible. But this view's even better." We've reached the end of the walkway. He scans an ID card on a retractable belt clip and opens the door to reveal an office decked out in shades of forest green, mint, and mahogany.

I gasp. Opposite us, another wall of glass showcases the lake. This evening, the water catches the waning sunlight. It's a dark blue, almost navy, with tinges of pink at the edges of the sand. Longdale Lake never looks the same. There are always subtle differences each and every day, and I have about a thousand photos on my phone to prove it.

"Your office? I'm surprised Sebastian didn't want this prime space."

"Oh, his is even bigger. Same view, just one floor above us." He eyes me curiously again and I wonder why. Can he see the dry shampoo powder residue in my peachalicious hair?

I run my hand through it again as I ooh and aww over all the gadgets he has, like the mechanical paperweight that actually gets up and walks off the paper when you don't need to weigh it down. It's literally a walking rock, sleek, not silly like you'd think.

Ridiculous, but so Oliver.

"Let me show you the space we've designated as the library," he says, but then he stops short.

"Oh, I almost forgot. I got you something." He walks back to his desk drawer and tugs it open.

"I only want it if it's a walking paperweight."

He snickers and hefts out a package. It looks heavy. He hands it to me. "Open it."

He's brought me little gifts before from places they've built their resorts, or places he's traveled to. Oliver leads a charmed life. And I'm happy for the Tates. I'm reminded again that my idea of a charmed life is eating a convenience portion of pot pie with my sister, Claire, while we watch *New Girl* episodes for the tenth time.

It's not that I don't want to travel or even move. Sometimes that seems nice, especially after Oliver sends me a photo of some sophisticated dish in Paris. But I promised my mom I'd take care of Claire, and I can't bear the thought of leaving the house behind.

I rip open the beige packaging, realizing there's a layer of bubble wrap protecting it. After finally getting that off—there's a reason librarians don't have long nails—I see it's a book with an exquisite, black brocade cover.

This man knows the way to my heart.

"A coffee table book?" I squeal out the words. It smells old. My favorite kind of book smell. "It's vintage?" My gaze travels to his and he gives a slight nod.

Did I imagine his swallow just now?

I run my hand over the raised cover and inhale, letting my eyes close briefly.

"Does it pass the book smell test?" he asks.

I nod and inhale again before taking a moment to read the title. *Libraries of Italy.* I open it, the spine cracking as if it hasn't been opened in a long time. Not only is it a *book* all about libraries, but it's also decades old, published in 1953.

"It shows us what the libraries looked like in Italy in the fifties?" My voice squeaks again.

Seriously, Oliver needs to stop doing this. He needs to stop buying me gifts that make it nearly impossible for another man to compete with.

I swallow hard. "Thank you."

He nods again and grabs my hand. "Come see the library area!"

I shouldn't do it. I shouldn't say yes to curating the library. Even though they'd be hard pressed to find someone better suited—for some reason, most of my self-esteem comes from knowing I'm a boss where books are concerned—I know it's a recipe for disaster.

Because I like Oliver. I like him like *that*. And every time he comes back into my life, even for a couple of hours at the shake shop, I'm reminded. No matter how many times I tell myself he can't mean anything to me, I'm caught up again.

We leave the office and head down the hall. Several yards past the other end of the third-floor balcony, I squeeze his hand, his gift tucked against my chest with my other arm. I go against my better judgment. "Let's do this. Let's curate the heck out of this library of yours."

His eyebrows rise and his mouth makes an O. "You'll do it?" He side hugs me and then presents the area for the library. "Here it is."

Claustrophobia claws at my throat. I'm confused. This can't be right.

I smile, my eyes are wide. But inside, I don't understand how I can possibly make this work.

Chapter 6

Oliver

I don't know what's worse. The look on Sophie's face when I show her the library nook or the look on her face when Sebastian walks up.

Both remind me of that *Tom and Jerry* cartoon when Tom the cat is so mad he turns red. You can see it happening—her face going from her normal, light shade to something closer to the beets our chef, Lionel, puts in my salad sometimes. Sophie is Tom reincarnate.

It's not like Sophie's necessarily mad, per se. At least I hope not. I guess she's disappointed in both the space and in seeing Sebastian again.

Because after she sees the library area, she barely has any time to recover the thinness of her lips and the red flush across her throat before Sebastian sucks up all the wind out of the room with his presence. And there go her cheeks and lips again. Once again like Tom's.

Maybe Sophie's red because she's glad to see him. I don't really know because the moment I see her blush at him, I find myself suddenly very occupied with the parking lot four floors down.

"Sophie," Sebastian says in his signature gravelly voice, his head tipping in her direction. A lot of women dig that whole blustery, "I'm wind chapped and grumpy" persona Sebastian has cultivated.

Cultivated? He was born this way—with a scowl. In every baby picture of him, his little forehead is wrinkled and he's looking at the camera like "Sigh. Pictures again? But I'll be late for my diaper change and scheduled tummy time."

I give him a hard time because I consider it my duty to keep him humble. But when push comes to shove—and there's been a lot of pushing and shoving amongst the Tates over the years—he's my brother and I admire him. He not only took Tate International to what it is today, but he's also the one who taught me how to tie a necktie and dribble a basketball.

Underneath the cold exterior, there's a good heart in there. I just doubt most people have seen evidence of it.

And like I was saying, the ladies are drawn to him. If his dollar bills in the bank don't attract them enough, then his Mr. Darcy approach to life sure does.

It didn't ever really bother me, this ability that Sebastian had to break hearts left and right, until it was Sophie's turn to crush on him. That's when I took personal offense to it.

But that's neither here nor there. Because it was a long time ago and I don't have any claim on Sophie or her heart.

That doesn't mean I can stand watching her gawk at my brother, though. And is he gawking back? I know she looks unreal in that dress of hers—sexy because it clings to her in all the best places, yet shy with the cute collar and sleeves.

Which is why I turn my attention back to the mostly empty parking lot. I can't do this right now.

She sees him and does a slight giggle cough thing in the back of her throat. I don't think I've ever heard that before. Leave it to Sebastian to be the catalyst for a new Sophie sound.

How soon can I redirect her back to the conversation at hand? The part where she's obviously concerned about the library nook. Except I'm not sure I want to revisit that either. Instead, I have to hear the back and forth between them and it's like nails scratching against every paper cut I've ever had.

"Sebastian, it's been a long time," Sophie says in a voice that's heavy with nerves. "This resort is off the hook."

And then she clears her throat again, and I have to stifle a laugh. *Off the hook?* Does anyone say that anymore? This makes me want to both laugh and cry.

"Thank you," Sebastian says. "I heard something about a petition for a new library? I figured you'd be involved with that."

"Yes. I've been working on it for awhile. We finally got the required number of signatures. Now we're just waiting to hear about the possibilities."

So, I lift my head from the riveting adventure that is the empty parking lot below and muster a smile. "How do you feel about the possibility of retiring Scott?" I put my arm around her shoulder and give a little side hug, which may or may not be because I'm feeling slightly territorial.

Sebastian's eyebrows go up, but his mouth stays in his permanent frown. "Scott?"

"It's my little nickname for the mobile library." Sophie giggles. "And I'll still get to keep him for a long while yet. These things take forever. If the county approves it, there will be a bond election in the fall, and then we'll go from there."

Her smile is looking a little droopy around the edges. Her gaze skitters to mine and there's something there, like she's asking me to relieve this discomfort.

I'll do anything to help Sophie avoid a prolonged exposure to my brother, so I turn to the nook, my hands spread wide. "I was just showing Sophie the space we've saved for the library. We're waiting on the shelving to come in. Should be any day now, right?" I look at Sebastian, willing him to answer quickly and go away.

Thankfully, he starts to leave. "Any day now," he says. He glances at Sophie, and I can tell that burst of surprise on his face—at how gorgeous Sophie is—is now covered by his usual mask. "Nice to see you again, Sophie. With your experience, we'd love any insights you might be able to give us for the library."

Sebastian gives a slight wave of his downturned hand and heads away, his mind already on another subject.

I speak up. "That's actually why she's here. I've invited her to be our consultant and curator for the library."

Sebastian turns halfway around, his eyes not meeting mine. He offers a second-long smile and a nod, but I know he's not happy with me. I don't often hire people without his consent, but hey, if he wants me in charge of operations at this resort, he needs to get used to me going off script sometimes.

Sophie is visibly more relaxed after Sebastian leaves and it has me wondering, with a rock in my chest, if that's because she still has feelings for him. If there's anything I have clear in my mind, it's that I would never want to be second fiddle to Sebastian, at least not in this way.

Except, it's a moot point because nothing is going to happen between Sophie and me.

I shore up my resolve to not let her and her endearing and confusing qualities affect me, and instead rotate to the other matter at hand.

"I—" I wonder how to phrase it. "I know the space is pretty small…"

Her lips perk up in a smile. "No, it's good!" She steps towards the bare wall and sweeps her hand across it. Then she turns to the wall of windows off the balcony and looks again at the view.

"It's fine that it's small. It's quaint and cozy. There might only be room for a couple of side chairs and a coffee table here, in front of the shelving units." She taps her closed lips with a finger, her other arm wrapped around her middle.

"Right. And the view is sort of embarrassing." I shrug, but soften my voice. "Wish we could have put it on the other side of the building with the lake views."

She steps toward the windows. "The parking lot isn't as appealing as the lake," she agrees. Her eyes are big and her arm gestures amplified. "But we'll make do. It's going to be great. Really."

She seems sincere, but I know her well enough to know there's an underlayer of disappointment.

"I'm sure, with your help, it will turn out. And I can ask Sebastian about possibly moving it." Why am I bringing up the brother I'll never measure up to? I guess I like pouring lemon juice on those roughed-up papercuts.

Besides, he runs a tight ship. Every inch of the resort has been spoken for since the planning stages.

"It's okay. I can maximize the space. I've been doing that with Scott for years." She gives a crooked smile. "I'm up for the challenge." And the way she's looking at me gives me the impression that she's talking about more than the nook. Or am I reading into it?

The silence stretches out, and I hate it. She and I always had a good connection. Something different. At times, back in the day, we were so comfortable it felt like cousins.

But now? It's nothing like cousins. I can't get her out of my head. And I care way too much about what she thinks.

Which is a problem. It's unacceptable because she used to like Sebastian. And I can't do relationships with my schedule. I'm sort of her boss now, right? And she used to like Sebastian. And I'm leaving Longdale as soon as humanly possible. Oh, and just a friendly reminder to myself: she used to like Sebastian.

"I'm excited," she says. She places a hand on my shoulder. "I'll be pushing for it to be really nice. I'm talking as high end as the budget will allow. The resort is so luxurious. You don't want to go chintzy here."

Using the word "chintzy" in the same sentence as Tate International is not okay. I'm starting to feel like Sebastian with this Longdale Lake project, all protective.

"Nothing associated with Tate International has been or ever will be chintzy. Geez, Soph."

"I'm not calling it 'chintzy.' Yet." Her gaze teases me.

"We have a certain pride, you know."

"Oh, I know that. You Tates and your pride." She starts walking down the corridor and I have to scramble to keep up. "Sebastian's the worst in that way, obviously. But I've always felt you were second worst. Or maybe Henry."

"If you think Sebastian is the most prideful, why were you in love with him all those years?"

I'm dangling bait in front of her face, and that doesn't feel right. I just somehow want to resolve this ache that wonders if she'd ever choose me over him. Not that any choosing of any kind will be happening.

She stops, one ankle warbling in those heels. "I never loved Sebastian." Her eyes are on fire.

"You hoped it was Sebastian working at the shake shop. I saw your face when it turned out to be me and not him."

She sighs and pinches her nose. "Really? This is so juvenile. It's how many years later? I didn't even know Sebastian. I still don't. You're the one I hung out with every day of the summer for three years. You're the one I've been friends with ever since then."

"I didn't imagine the pout." Even now, it hits me. And she's right—it is juvenile. But it's like that part of my brain never grew out of it. And maybe, in some weird way, I want her to admit her feelings for him. Then that would prevent me from getting out of hand with these strange feelings *I'm* having for *her*.

"The pout? What, like this?" She takes a step towards me and pulls her lips down, just a little. The bottom lip juts out and it's a pink, sweet blossom. I want it. I want to kiss her whole mouth.

"Yes, like that," I manage.

We stand there, a magnetism unlike anything I've ever felt going between us.

And that's when I wise up and decide to extricate myself from this confusing situation.

I run a hand through my hair and shoot out a breath. "I've got a meeting to get to. Can you come back tomorrow? We should probably order the books soon."

She takes a step back and runs her tongue over her lips. "Yeah." She swallows hard. "I close up my big ole bus at around six. I can come after that."

I give her an awkward "thanks" and then, in an act of self-defense, I head back to my office.

"Can you find your way out?" I turn to ask before I'm too far down the hall. She's still standing there, looking at the blank space with wonder in her eyes, like she's already dreaming up possibilities.

"I'll—I'll be fine, Oliver," she says, not looking at me.

It's said with resolve, and I wonder if she means she'll be fine in more ways than just navigating her way out of the building.

I hope she does mean that. I hope we're both "fine" enough to see this little arrangement through without damage to our friendship.

"Good," I say.

Because she has to understand one thing. I care about her, I do. But I'm never settling down, especially with someone who used to be in love with my brother.

Chapter 7

Sophie

I spend my morning in Tollark, where I dress up in regency dress for my ladies' book club. We set up lawn chairs in a circle outside of Scott in the Kroger parking lot so we can best corral the moms' toddlers. With all that going on, it's easy for me to not think about my disappointment over the resort library's lack of space and good views.

It's okay. I can do this.

In the afternoon in Fairhill, it's harder to keep my mind off of it. I vacillate between pure excitement and dread. It didn't help that we only had seven patrons, not counting Violet's mother who ended up taking a nap against the stacks.

Which was fine because then Violet could dish on her recent tour of several independent bookstores across the country. It was chronicled on her Bookstagram account to great success, but I wanted to get the real info:

how things went with the guy her mom convinced to go with her at the last minute.

From her rush of whispered, detailed descriptions of their transcontinental adventures, it seems my twenty-something employee had a *fabulous* time.

Which I'm happy about. Violet deserves love as much as anyone. I'm not against love.

I'm against falling for the man who can only break my heart.

After such a scintillating day, I head home to shower and change.

My sister, Claire, was already home from her city administrator job. "*New Girl* binge tonight?" she asks through the door while I'm in my room deciding what to wear. "Or do you want to go crazy and rewatch season one of *The Mandalorian*?"

"You're on your own tonight, Claire," I say through the shirt I'm trying to pull over my head, the fabric sticking to my mouth. "I'm going up to Tate International." I squeeze my eyes shut, bracing myself for her reaction.

There is none, which is suspicious. I haven't said anything to her about running into Oliver two days ago, or about the time I spent with him yesterday. And I most certainly haven't mentioned his job offer.

I finish getting dressed and go find her in our little kitchen, which we've been trying to remodel for years. I glance at the half-done, coral subway tile backsplash. It's going to look great...eventually. Maybe the income from working with Oliver will speed up the process.

"Tate? As in, Oliver?" I know Claire's staring at me, but I busy myself by rummaging around the contents of our refrigerator.

"Tate, as in, the company that builds resorts," I correct. I take a deep breath. May as well go for it, like a band-aid, right off. "They hired me to curate their resort library." I refrain from telling her about my disappointment in its size.

"What? When?" She stares at me open-mouthed. Even though she's younger than me, she's the taller one. Her nose is longer and more graceful. Her hair is curly like mine, but a lighter shade of brown.

I grab a bag of baby carrots and turn to her.

"He saved me from Troy's dad." I laugh as I finally break, telling her about his catching me crawling on my hands and knees, about riding in his car, and that Troy's father finally found us.

"I'm so glad you said no about chairing Longdale Days, Soph. That would have been a nightmare—for me, mostly."

"I wouldn't have asked you to do much." Even as I say it, I know that's not fully true.

Claire gives me a look that reminds me of a warden telling an inmate not to touch the glass partition between the calling booths. "I've lived with you when you've had projects like that. It's a nightmare."

"Well, you're in luck because I said no."

"Troy's dad is just...yuck."

"Agreed."

"I'm glad you gave up the bad habit that was Troy."

I am, too. More than I can express. But that doesn't mean I'm happy about Claire's negative comments about him the entire time we were dating. She was right, but it would have been nice to get support from her, regardless of her personal feelings about Troy.

"So, Oliver just up and asked you to work for him, huh?"

"Temporarily. It's not a big deal." I wave her away and stuff my mouth full of a ranch-dipped carrot.

The tilt of Claire's head tells me she's not buying that. "Please keep your wits about you."

I choose naivete. "My wits? I'm not going to blow the budget over graphic novels and board books." I'm back in the fridge, grabbing a couple of slices of turkey from the deli bag.

"That's not what I mean, and you know it." Now Claire's got her arms crossed over her chest. Her voice is soft. She reminds me of mom in this pose, level-headed, bossy, but with a gentle demeanor that makes it impossible for me to be mad at her for too long. I almost wish she'd get upset or something. Then it would be easier to feel justified in my frustration.

When I don't respond on account of the turkey I'm devouring, she carries on. "Many a woman has had a hard time being...smart...around the Tate men. You deserve better, Sophie. Oliver Tate can't give you what you need."

I sigh and squeeze my eyes shut. "And what is it you think I need, Claire?"

The sound of her voice tells me she's stepped closer to me. "A stable man who appreciates you and...all your...quirks." That last word is said louder and at a higher pitch.

That's what I want. Of course I do. I'm pretty sure that's what my mom wanted, too. But she didn't get it. She got a man who turned out to be unstable. He didn't appreciate or want her, or my sister, or me.

And after the debacle that was Troy, I'm not sure I can trust myself. I was heading straight down that road with him that was devoid of the sorts of feelings I'd always knew—innately—I deserved. I was fixing to commit without that real and abiding feeling of love. What kind of woman does that? Someone who can't be trusted to make good decisions about herself and her own life, that's who.

Add in my persistent attraction to Oliver and I'm really, really not trusting myself these days.

But I can't say all of this to Claire right now. We're both in a mood. "Noted." I give one nod, take a last bite of turkey, and step into the mud room to put on my shoes: my old Mary Janes, a scuffed, dull red.

"And you're going to this new temporary job wearing these clothes, why? You look like you're ready to go to work in a factory…" She glances at my feet. "In odd, used-to-be nice shoes."

I shudder but tell myself to stick to my resolve and not change out of my old, baggy jeans. "First you tell me not to fall for the Tates and then you mock my choice of clothing designed to help me not fall for them?" I snort and sling my little canvas bag that doubles as a purse over my shoulder.

Claire's hair swings around as she goes to open the door for me. "Gotcha. If you're going for the look that says, 'please don't notice me,' you've made the perfect choice."

"Thanks," I say, not at all thankful about this conversation, but glad to be leaving it behind.

I get in my gray-blue Toyota Corolla and start it up, looking down at my old, mom-waisted jeans and plain, long-sleeved tee.

The dress I'd worn last time was too much. It had a nice cut—one of my best dresses. What had I been thinking? I can't do that sort of thing. I can't lose my head.

Thus, the most boring, shapeless outfit I could find.

Something had come over Oliver yesterday. It was like he'd been holding his breath and then had that panicked feeling like he needed to come up for air. We went from standing there, arguing about my old feelings surrounding Oliver being hired instead of Sebastian, to him leaving, doing some weird waving thing at me as he walked down the hall.

I'll admit it. I had been jonesing for Sebastian when Oliver started working there. I was good and sad for one, maybe two shifts. But then, it was like something clicked and the immature crush on his older brother was erased. By the time I was good and mature—at eighteen years old—I'd fully and wholeheartedly said a secret "I do" to seal my heart to Oliver.

I read a lot of books, okay? I'm dramatic sometimes.

But Oliver used to feel like my other half. Like a guy who both finishes your sentences and points out the spinach in your teeth, all while making you feel like a million bucks.

I felt nothing for Sebastian when he walked in the room yesterday. I haven't for a very long time.

It was the way Oliver was looking at me that had my stomach batting away butterflies. First, he studied me and my reactions to Sebastian. Then, he looked at me when I pouted and the energy in the room made my knees soft—useless. The way he stared at my lips? In a different life, I would have grabbed him and kissed him senseless.

It was a good thing he walked away.

Chapter 8

Sophie

Except for the security guard who nods when I arrive at the resort, I don't see anyone else here. Even when I step out of the elevator, the fourth floor feels empty and quiet. I walk past Oliver's closed office door and down the hall.

I reach the library nook area. Yes, it's miniscule. But with the right finishings and décor, it will turn out, right?

Unsure if I should go knock on Oliver's office door, I start looking at photos of hotel libraries on my phone. Most seem at least twice the size of this little...area. I can't even call it a room. Oliver's probably right, though. Sebastian's not going to budge on this. And I'm not about to look a gift horse in the mouth.

My eyes scan the area, my mind filling in the spaces with possibilities. Maybe the Tates would let me put up some luxurious drapes and add some greenery, to define the space a little better.

One thing is certain, I will make this work. This is an opportunity I will not squander. Don't get me wrong. I love my main squeeze, Scott, the mobile library—he feels like home. But I've been working there a long time, cramped, dealing with the smell of antifreeze, needing to conjure some silly song and dance to drum up interest in the library as I drive it from town to town.

But this? Curating a library for the Tate brothers' resort? I've been in a tight, stuffy desert and Oliver's bringing me a tall glass of water.

Oliver himself is a tall glass of water, but that's a whole other story…one that I can't crack open and dive into, even though I want to.

I wait around for a few more minutes before heading back down the way I came. I rap on his office door, imagining how amazing it would be to take it off its hinges, widen the doorway a bit, and put the library in here.

He opens it and is on the phone. His eyes grow large, and he grins. He puts his hand over his phone and whispers to me, "Hey, come on in. Stella's here at the resort, but she's kind of lost." He leaves the door open behind me.

"Aunt Stella?" I squeal. "She's here at the hotel?" Oliver's dad's sister is one of a kind. I met Oliver's parents once at Shake, Shake, Shake, and nearly broke out in hives from trying to avoid any foot-in-my-mouth scenarios or spilling their shakes all over them.

But Stella is warm and gentle. She could make Monaco royalty feel comfortable at a Longdale barn dance.

"She's trying to find us," he whispers, and then gets back to Stella, giving her directions to turn left and then right. To be fair, the layout is confusing, and most of the doors and hallways don't have any signs on them yet.

Pretty soon, Stella's there and she's hugging me in a cloud of almond lotion scent, and maybe some of whatever food she brought in a Pyrex container.

"Sophie!" She looks at me, then at Oliver, and then back at me. "I'm glad to see you two hanging out again." She has big hair—a short, chic steel grey style that's been teased and sprayed. Her large, blue eyes hold a genuine sweetness. She lives just a few streets over from me and was the Longdaler who helped the most when my mom died.

"I still can't believe these boys are building this thing in Longdale," she says to me as she touches Oliver's cheek. "I would have never predicted they'd do such a thing, being so busy conquering the world. But I couldn't be happier about it. With this place to tend to, we'll get the boys here in town more often." With that, she gives his cheek a light smack.

The Tate brothers visited their aunt every summer growing up. It was her house they flocked to, while their parents were in some foreign country, doing charity work or something or other to build the family business. All the boys love her, especially Oliver.

He reaches over for a Stella hug around the Pyrex. "Glad you found my office. I was beginning to wonder if you would," he teases.

"It's not my fault this thing is a maze." Stella holds out a hand. "It's gorgeous." Her gaze flits around the room. "But it's so over the top that my head is spinning."

"Only the best for Longdale Lake, Stella." Oliver eyes the Pyrex before reaching over to try to peel the lid off. "Did you bring me food?"

She bats his hand away and he laughs. "It's for you, Alec and Sebastian." She turns to me. "And Sophie, of course. Beef stew. I made too much. Besides, I haven't been over in a while." She takes in the room again. "Things are coming together," she says with a twinkle in her eye.

Her two children are older than all the Tate boys, nearly out of the house when her husband passed away and her nephews started coming for their summer visits. The Tate boys are more like her own children than nephews.

We chitchat, Stella asking me about the mobile library and if we had a title she's interested in—a popular memoir.

"With any luck, within a year or two, you'll be able to visit us at a permanent location...somewhere," I tell her.

"I heard the petition got enough signatures finally," Stella says. "Congratulations, Sophie. We need something bigger and better than the bus. Imagine how much nicer your job would be in an actual building."

I allow myself one second to hope, imagining rows and rows of stacks, every title we could ever want brightening up the space.

Oliver cuts in. "Sophie's agreed to curate and design our hotel library here."

Stella lights up. "That's wonderful. You better pay her for her time and talents, Oliver."

I *did* have time and talent where libraries were concerned.

"We're paying her." Oliver's response reminds me a little of when Stella would visit the shake shop and she'd remind him to say thank you to the customers or that he needed to move his clean clothes to the dryer when he got home.

"I was thinking it might be cool if we had a guest book for the library. With a fancy pen and a ribbon bookmark," I tell her. "And the guests could add in their favorite books and then the hotel could purchase them to add it to the collection and add in a nameplate on the inside front cover. You know, the guest's first name and where they live."

Oliver regards me with surprise. "That's a good idea. It would personalize things. And give a little something extra when they come back."

I nod, my mind turning over the possibilities. "And maybe we could include books from local authors. I know there are at least two who write books with Longdale Lake as the setting."

"Maybe we should hire you on full time, since you have all these amazing ideas." Oliver's eyes brand me. He's complimenting me again and I fall for it—again. It's like he's read through my list of insecurities and fears and he's single-handedly taking them on, one by one.

Give Sophie validation in the form of a library job.

Check.

Speak words that make her feel seen and heard.

Check. Check.

Look at her with wonder, even in mom pants and scuffed shoes.

Check. Check. Check.

"That's a perfect plan, Sophie." Stella rests a hand on my arm. "Oh, and Henry was telling me about a really good book he was reading. What was it called? I think it was a new epic fantasy."

I was just about to say which title she might be referring to, but Oliver interrupts.

"You spoke with Henry? When?" His mouth has gone slack.

"Oh, well, a few days ago." She shrugs.

"Why did he call you?" Oliver has a vein in his forehead that usually lies dormant and invisible. But there are times when it comes out to play. Right now? It's a pulsing beast, taunting anyone who comes near.

Stella's gaze darts around the room, and then it meets mine, like she's wondering why it's such a big deal. "He calls me every other week, maybe. I don't know." She moves to an overstuffed chair. "He likes to check in…make sure I'm okay and that I get the things he sends to me."

"He sends you things?" both Oliver and I ask at the exact moment.

I pipe up to say, "Jinx!" but the word dies off before I can finish it. Oliver isn't having any of this. His concern is palpable.

"Oh, it's just things I need that I forget to buy. Like a can of winterizer to put in my car." She laughs. "A timer for the hoses in that section of my lawn that's just out of reach of my sprinkler system. It's so nice that I don't have to go outside and pull the hose around."

Oliver's looking at her like she's lost her mind. "You never told me he keeps in touch with you."

"Is that a problem?" She glances at me and then back to Oliver, her eyes narrowing. "He's been doing it for a long time. And he always has some cute story about Navie to share, but I don't think he gets to see her too often, sadly. He mails her stuff more often than he mails me stuff."

Oliver swallows hard. "Do you know where he's living now?"

Stella looks up, scrunching her nose. "I want to say Crete? Or maybe he's staying somewhere else for awhile before going back to Crete. I don't know. He doesn't mention much about where he is." She shrugs. "I know his security job is hush hush."

Before Oliver can ask more questions, she changes the subject and turns to me.

"Have Patricia and Vernon forgiven the Tates for ruining their plans?" She's asking it sincerely, and I'm taken back by her concern. My grandparent's plans for filling the valley with wind turbines to cut down on city power costs was a divisive subject. Many people in town were happy, or at least satisfied, when the Tate brothers came in with their resort idea. Hundreds of trees were saved, too. There are others who still wish for lower power bills, though. And my grandparents suffered financially after all that went down.

I cock my head to one side. "They're making peace with it."

It was true, the sting of the Tates sweeping in with their money and upending their bid for the property had subsided in my grandparents over the last three years. Grandpa's ashen coloring and slumped shoulders are nowhere to be found these days. At least most of the time.

But they still wouldn't like it one bit if they knew I was going to consult for the Tates. Oh, I love the way the term "consultant" makes me feel. I should add that to my Linked In profile.

Validate Sophie's work and the importance of it.

Check. Check. Check. Check.

My grandparents have no idea about the rendezvous at Shake, Shake, Shake every year since the age of eighteen. And they don't know I'm here now.

It's okay, I tell myself. I can do whatever suits my fancy. Even if it means hanging out with Oliver Tate in this "gross monstrosity," as my grandparents call it.

They've got it all wrong, though. The resort is built to the highest standards of ecological care and concern. It's an asset to the area, anyone with eyeballs can see that. But that doesn't mean I'll share that I'm working for Oliver.

"I'm glad they're coming to terms with it," Stella says. "Even though they don't live here anymore, I know it was a hard setback to lose that bid."

The Tates and the Hansons—head to head. And now I'm consorting with the enemy.

Oliver scowls. I'm sure hearing the Hanson name has the same effect on him as their hearing his name has on them.

He holds up his palms. "Sophie and I've managed to be pretty much Switzerland on this, haven't we, Soph?"

"Yes, we have. I think we've been very mature."

Stella glances back and forth between the two of us. I'd bet she'd be happy with our union.

Our "union?" I've got to stop thinking of words like that when I'm around Oliver. And all words that indulge my long-running feelings.

"I'd better go," Stella says. "The dogs will be anxious for their evening walk." She says goodbye, but not before gathering me in another hug and calling me "beautiful."

Where my grandparents are formal and at arms' length, everything about Stella is sunny. She accepts me as I am.

Oliver hugs her, too.

But Stella's words about my grandparents' pride niggle at the back of my brain. And I can't very well talk to Oliver about it. Hello, conflict of interest!

When she's gone, I sign the freelance contract paperwork and he tells me he has to speak with human resources. "You can hang out in my office until I get back. Take a nap on the sofa...I've dozed off a time or two. It's so soft."

I shake my head. "I'll just find a space in the lobby to sit." I can't very well hang out here. I have to be the consummate professional. "I'd like to start pulling together some ideas for titles to order."

"I'm really happy you'll be working on this for us, Sophie." He draws near me, and I find myself leaning into him. He smells so good, the cedarwood and pear filling my nose and head.

"Anything for a friend," I say, straightening my t-shirt and turning to the door. My voice is cheery, casual. But to my ears, it sounds foreign and hollow.

I tell him I'll be in the lobby and then I leave, not looking back.

Chapter 9

Oliver

It's almost six o'clock in the evening, and instead of finishing my work and going over to hang out with Alec at his house near the resort or—shudder—going home to my rental alone, I'm waiting for Sophie.

She comes to the resort most evenings after she finishes at the mobile library, talking a mile a minute about whatever the adventure du jour was. I have a hard time keeping a straight face through her stories—and I strongly suspect she likes making me laugh. Sometimes she goes on and on about how Mrs. So-and-so gossiped about someone else she thinks I should remember. Usually, I don't.

Other times, she tells me about a shipment of books like they're rare chocolates imported from Bavaria. I wonder if she's going to love her future children as much as she loves her books.

And that's when I shoot out a relieved breath that she's not going to be having kids with her ex, Troy. That she was almost engaged to him sobers me like nothing else.

I took her for granted before. I can admit that. I should probably admit it to her—and apologize. But now we're in this strange dance of sort-of-boss, sort-of-employee, and I haven't yet figured out how to go about things.

I'm going to figure this out, though. And so far, we've kept things professional between us.

It isn't easy, but it's absolutely necessary.

Sophie and I are too different to be together. I've always known this. I just have to hold out for a few more months and then I'll be in Capri. I can't make any rash moves that might jeopardize my goals. Yeah, I'm drawn to Sophie more and more, but I love my career scouting for Sebastian.

Being in Longdale hasn't been easy for me. I can't seem to settle in. There's just something about it that feels a little off. And, go figure, Sophie will never leave Longdale.

I'm happy she's doing this job for us—I'm sure she can use the money and we need her experience. But maybe I moved without thinking things through. Because it's going to hurt a heck of a lot more to leave her in a few months than it ever did to leave her each August.

With a groan, I wander out of my office. Unlike Sebastian, who's most comfortable in a boardroom, I have to take frequent breaks. I pad down the hall to the elevator. Might as well wait for her down in the lobby and walk her up.

Before the elevator doors open on the ground floor, my phone dings with a text. Sebastian's asking a question about the business. I growl my ir-ritation. He's a workaholic and has a habit of calling impromptu meetings right when I'm ready to head home. I want to help Sophie, not be pelted with questions and demands from my older brother.

By "help Sophie," I totally mean watch her face light up as she gets excited about every little strange or random thought that comes to mind. And, to be clear, I'm watching her face in a completely "friends only" way.

I reach the lobby, waiting for her to appear at the main entrance when another text from Sebastian comes through. *Where are you?*

Great. He's looking for me now. He has access to all the security cameras right on his phone, so it's going to take him a matter of seconds to find me.

I'm a little out of breath as I reach the front doors, a thrill zipping through me as I see Sophie walking up the front way. She has on a light blue dress that fans out at the bottom. It swings with every step she takes, and I stare at her legs for a moment before I come to my senses.

"Perfect timing, Soph," I tell her. I laugh as an idea strikes me. "You've got to save me." I reach for her hand and, glancing around the lobby, we walk-run across the slate and marble floor, past the front desk, and through a seating area out to the back terrace.

The hand holding? It's only because I'm asking her to run and this floor is slick. That's it.

She's laughing. "What am I saving you from?" she asks, glancing behind us at the back doors that have yet to slide closed. "Sebastian looks ticked."

Crap. I turn my head to see him standing at the door, his arms crossed over his chest.

I pick up the pace. "We're running from him, of course he's ticked," I say.

She slows down to kick her heeled shoes off her feet, paying little attention to where they land. I do the same, making a show of flinging my

Italian loafers wildly. She rewards me with a shrieking laugh. One of mine disappears into a small bush. I cringe because all the vegetation on our grounds was planted only recently. I strip off my socks and chuck them behind a tree.

"And why are we running from him?" she asks, placing the hand I'm not holding over her heart. "If I'd known, I would have brought my sneakers." I'm not sure, but it sounds like she whispers, "...and a sports bra," to herself.

A smile scratches at my lips, but I don't want to embarrass her by commenting further. "His questions can wait," I say. "You're here." I don't dare look back because I'm sure that Sebastian is either standing there, fuming, or chasing after us, and I don't want to see either. Instead, I train my focus on the lake. The sun, low on the horizon, is shining brilliantly across the water.

Her laugh is throaty, her head thrown back to the sky.

We reach the end of the terrace, and I make an executive decision. "This way," I say. I switch directions, running across the grass to the dock.

We reach my boat. My gorgeous, new rowboat—all whiskey-soaked teak, oil rubbed, perfect. I haven't had a chance to take it out yet. Right now, with Sophie, is as good a time as any.

I let go of her hand so I can grab the painter and toss it into the water. It slaps the lake with a pelting sound, and just like that, my heart starts to pound even more than when we were running. I love my new boat. And I love rowing. And adding Sophie to the mix? It's pure heaven.

I motion to the bench seats padded with ivory leather. Yeah, I went all out on this purchase. But I've got to take advantage of it now before the busy summer season, before motorboats and jet skis descend here like seagulls on a vat of worms.

She's still standing on the boat slip, hesitating. I don't remember her having a fear of the water or boats before. We used to go out with other shake shop employees after our shift. No, it's not a fear of boats or water that's in those golden-brown eyes. It's something else. I offer my hand, but she ignores it, stepping into the boat without assistance, easing herself down on the padded bench.

"Go!" she screams. I push off and grab both oars in the oarlocks. She wobbles at the force, circling her hands to keep from falling off the bench.

Now that we're in the water, I crane my neck to find Sebastian. Sure enough, he's standing in the grass, his hands at his hips. I can't see his face, but I'd bet the entire Tate International fortune that he's frowning. My phone vibrates yet again, and I stop rowing so I can see his text. *Real mature, Oliver.*

I show Sophie and she giggles.

I slide my phone back into my pocket and begin rowing again, this time for real, as I get into the motion.

It's my flow state. It's unity of all the good things. Warm sun, water, a boat that glides like a hot knife through butter. And the view of Sophie? I can't get over the way her dress is perfectly fitted on top and how it swings out from her waist. I'm distracted by her legs that somehow look longer against the fabric of the dress. They're not tanned, they're fair like the rest of her. Lately, I've found the contrasts between her dark brown hair and white skin alluring. She used to complain about her inability to tan—how her legs were pasty white.

I can't believe I didn't notice back then that they weren't pasty, they're luminous and toned. Like the surface of a creamy pearl.

Her hair is wild, coming out of a clip in the back because of the wind.

"Want me to take a turn?" she asks, pointing to the oars.

I shake my head but offer a smile. I don't mean to be possessive here, but I'm not ready to relinquish my baby to anyone yet, not even Sophie.

We're quiet for awhile, the solitude yawning lazily before us. "So, why were we running from Sebastian?" she asks. "Is he going to fire us now?"

I don't answer that. Instead, I'm caught on another, interesting observation. "You came with me, no questions asked."

She shrugs. "You saved me the other day when Troy's dad was hunting me down. I'm returning the favor." The breeze hits her face again. She plays with the bracelet on her wrist. "But seriously, what did he do that made you run? I'm an accessory to this crime. You owe me an explanation."

"You know Sebastian. He's too serious." I take in the slice of the oars through the water. "It's been a long day and I'm done. I keep telling him that taking breaks will only help his productivity, but he doesn't believe me." I gaze behind her at the mountain in the distance, the resort set so perfectly into the rise—like wood inlay. "Besides, I haven't been on the water since I got here. You're part of this beauty's maiden voyage."

"Really? I feel so special." She laughs, but then her mouth goes in a straight line as she looks at me. She clears her throat. "It has been a long time since you've been on the lake, then. Obviously, you didn't come out last August because you didn't come to town at all." Her back is straight. She's staring at me.

I only feel relief, because she finally seems open to discussing how and why I missed last year's closing night. I'm ready. She deserves as much—and more—from me.

Even though I know it's the right time to tell her this, I still hesitate. It's not going to be easy. There are a lot of aspects to this that have nothing to do with me, and I have to proceed with caution.

"Soph, I need to tell you why I didn't come."

Chapter 10

Oliver

The way the sunlight hits the water is giving me a headache. Suddenly, this picturesque setting is grating at me, and the place between my shoulder blades feels slick as my rowing has intensified.

I've been waiting, impatiently, for a chance to go out in the water. I may or may not have pictured Sophie sitting right here in this spot when I looked at photos of the boat online.

But now that we're out here, in the heat, I'm tired. It's not fair to Sophie to give her an abbreviated version of why I didn't come last year. I need to tell her everything that I'm at liberty to say.

I let out a breath and ship the oars. I pinch my face where it's starting to throb, right between my eyebrows.

"Alec needed me," I say. "He called me the day I was supposed to fly here and he was…" Even now, remembering the sound of his voice gives me chills. "…not okay."

I pause, the words getting stuck in my throat. Alec asked me not to tell people. Besides, until now, Sophie has shut down any of my attempts to talk about this.

I was a jerk, and she deserves an explanation. It's tricky because it's Alec's stuff. It's not exactly my story to tell.

"So you went to help him," she encourages.

"Yeah." I wish I could leave it at that, but that won't do. "I went to San Antonio."

She laces her hands together. "Really?"

"When I got there, it looked like he'd been in a fight. He had a big gash across his forehead and bandages over his hands."

Sophie gasps and covers her mouth. Remembering his swollen face, my stomach turns.

"He'd had an accident. And it happened about a week after he'd torn up his leg." I pause. "Did you know that his injury is called the unhappy triad? It's the worst knee injury to get—two ligaments and a meniscus are torn."

Sophie cringes. "Poor Alec. That's a fun fact I'll have to remember, the unhappy triad." Sophie gives a half-smile. "Not that it's 'fun,' of course." She's a trivia geek. She likes sharing strange but true tidbits with the kids who come into the library.

"And this accident was in addition to that?" she asks.

I nod. "Gabriel went out there to be with him after the knee injury, but when he had to go back home to Denver, Alec decided to try to drive."

"What made him think he could do that?" Sophie stares at me. She's intrigued. She's never been one to back down from finding answers about things. It's part of what makes her such a good librarian. Her mind is insatiable—when one question gets answered, three more crop up.

"He...wasn't in his right frame of mind." My voice betrays my apprehension in sharing more. "He wasn't supposed to mix his pain medication with anything stronger than an energy drink. But he did—" I cut myself off. I don't want to betray Alec's trust, but this is Sophie and I need her to understand why I had to go.

She nods, knowing what I'm getting at.

"Thankfully, the accident wasn't too bad. No one else was hurt. But he was scraped up, and his knee had been bumped, which set his recovery back."

"That's good it wasn't worse," she says. I can see the anguish in her eyes, and I know she cares.

"I was just about to fly into Denver from some scouting in New York when I got his call. He sounded miserable, and asked me not to tell anyone. I changed my flight to San Antonio."

I grip the oars again and row. "It was humiliating for him. Demoralizing. Here, he'd just been injured in a pre-season game, of all things. It was looking like it would possibly end his career because of its severity and because surgery didn't go like they'd hoped. And then Gabriel left, and Alec got to thinking about Callie."

Sophie swallowed hard. "The college girlfriend who died."

I can only nod. After a minute of tortured thought, I speak again. "He was depressed and out of it and wanted to take a drive to her gravesite...in Austin."

Her brows go up. "Austin's like, a couple of hours away from San Antonio, right?"

"Yeah. He only got a few miles into the trip before he swerved and hit a chain link fence. Thankfully not much damage to property since he was going slow. But...he was embarrassed. He ended up losing his license for a year."

"Sounds like you were exactly where you needed to be, Oliver." She gives a soft laugh and the sound of it carries over the swish of water.

I know she's right, but that doesn't mean I handled everything in the right way.

"I'm glad I went to help him. But Sophie, it was inconsiderate to not contact you sooner. And to not follow up was just—"

She's fidgeting with her hair clip now. The way she looks in that dress—it's the perfect amount of a little too tight—combined with her long curls is messing with my mind.

I suddenly forget all the reasons why I'm not supposed to fall for her.

"Oliver, it really helps to know why. It's okay."

We grow quiet, and I'm exhausted. The waves are in our favor now, and we've almost reached the other side. It's the uninhabited side. Owned by the government. It's quiet here and wild. Still untamed. Yeah, the sand's not great. It's got weeds and bugs. But I want to get there and sit on the beach, however rocky, with Sophie.

Sophie speaks up again. "It did bother me. And I thought, let's just play it cool. He's probably outgrown our little rendezvous."

"Outgrown? I'll never outgrow closing night." I rest the oars on my lap and reach over and touch her knee. Her dress just barely covers it, but a pang hits me. I wish I could trace her kneecap with my finger—her warm, bare skin beckons to me.

A thousand bad words form in my mind because I'm pining after Sophie Lawson's...kneecap?

She stares down at my hand. "Except you will outgrow it, because we can't keep doing this forever."

My chest burns with a truth I don't want to think about. She's right. She'll get married someday. Please for the love of all that's holy, don't let it be to Troy. Or to anyone even remotely like Troy.

I've fixated on him—I know that. I'm starting to figure out that maybe he's just a representation of something much larger at play in my mind here.

"Well, I'm not ready to give it up quite yet," I say. "Besides, I'll be living here still for this year's closing night. No worries there. And for next year's, I'm hoping there'll be cause for celebration since construction on our Capri resort better be underway. I'll definitely want to come and eat a milkshake with you."

Something simmers in her golden-flecked eyes, her irises lined with a darker brown. She's holding back, and alarm pricks up along my neck. If she wants to be done with closing night, I...I have to respect her wishes.

There's a shift in her expression as she leans forward and points past me. "It's the black ibis!" She stares, and I rest the oars and turn to look. There are three, with long, spindly legs, and black and maroon feathers. They're on the shore on the far side of the lake, which we're nearing now.

"So that's where they've gone," she says. And then, in a whisper, she adds, "I love their gracefully pointy beaks." Her voice is sweet, almost like a coo. It reminds me of how she talks to her dog, Wilford.

The wind picks up and her body tilts to one side. "Whoa!" She laughs, and then grips the bench on either side of her.

I take one pull of the oars before she gasps. "My bracelet!"

"Your what? What happened?"

She rotates to peer over the side of the boat. "I think my bracelet fell off when I saw the ibis."

"Ye lost yer wristlet in the drink?" I say, giving her my best pirate captain accent. "I'll fetch it for you, my lady."

"Your accent is way off. It's like Pirates of the Caribbean's Aussie little brother."

I laugh. "I should probably just stick to the Oliver accent from now on."

She gazes at me, her lips curled into a lazy smile. "No, I like the stupid accents. It's part of your charm."

"I have charm?" I can't help teasing her with a grin. Anytime she's nice like this, I have to draw it out.

"About this much, yes." She measures half an inch with her pointer finger and thumb.

I shake my head and move the oar in the water, peering in to try to find the bracelet.

"Was it gold? Silver?"

"It was diamond. Worth about twenty grand."

I glance at her in surprise, and she laughs. "I had to try. You might have felt bad enough to offer me some compensation."

"No way. You're the one who lost it."

"Or." She lifts a finger, her smile growing. "You could have dived in after it." She leans back on her hands, her eyes challenging me.

Before I can talk myself out of it, I remove my phone from my pocket and stow it beneath me. I take off my shirt. I'm shy for a second. Yeah, I lift weights and run on the beach on the resort side of the lake. I know I'm not bad to look at. But I've acknowledged to myself that I care what Sophie thinks of me.

"Wait." She starts laughing and then covers her mouth with both hands. "I wasn't serious, Oliver."

"Are you laughing at my body?" I stick my belly out to make it round and rub my hand over it like I'm pregnant. That's what I do. I make people laugh. And my favorite person to make laugh is Sophie.

She stands up carefully, widening her stance so she doesn't fall overboard. "No." Her expression is serious. "I'm definitely not laughing at your body." Her gaze sweeps over me for one brief moment before landing on my face again.

Mercy me, Sophie. You can't look at me like that.

We're in a standoff, playing chicken, the heat from her gaze reeling me in. I hate the plank of wood that's between us. I need to get closer to her at all costs.

I either step over this plank and kiss her, or dive in.

Without thought, I choose the safer, less confusing route and hate myself for it. I grunt as I hit the surface. The water is bone cold.

"Oliver, Oliver!" Her voice is panicked, and I can hear it even from my watery purgatory.

I rise up and get a breath of air. My skin already aches from the cold. I doggie paddle, whipping my head around for any sign of her bracelet.

"I'm. Fine. Just. Cold." I try to reassure her. We're in a shallow part near the shore opposite of the resort. I can easily swim ashore if I need to. No sign of the bracelet, though.

"You didn't. Tell. Me." I pause to breathe and try not to think about how I could have dived into a vat of snow and been warmer than I am right now. "What color. Your bracelet is."

"You didn't give me a chance." She's squeezing her cheeks with both palms, her eyes like saucers.

I plunge under again, opening my eyes. Nothing. I can make out some of the shapes at the bottom, and although it's dark, I see a mass of seaweed. Nothing resembles jewelry.

"Oliver, wait. Wait!" I hear her muffled voice and come up to the surface. She reaches out a hand to stop me from going under again. I try to smile, but I'm so paralyzed by the cold that it probably looks like the time my dad had Bell's Palsy for a little while.

"It was—" She holds up a gold bangle with one hand, and wraps her other hand over her middle, her shoulders slumping. "It was at the bottom of the boat." She bites her lip, her forehead crinkling. "I'm so sorry…"

You've got to be freaking kidding me. I feel like swearing. Not at Sophie, but at myself. If I'd been trying to impress her or win her over, at least I'd look like some kind of hero. But I'm not. I just feel like a fool who's going to die of frostbite to the lungs.

I nod, but again, the Bell's Palsy effect I've got going on makes it hard. Should I climb back in or just pull the boat to the shore?

"Remember that time we got stranded out here on the jet ski when it ran out of gas? I remember the crazy seaweed over here." She's leaning so far over the side of the boat, that I worry for her safety.

"Be careful there," I manage through the cold. "Don't want you to fall in."

She clicks her tongue and rolls her eyes. "I'm not going to fall in. This is not my first rodeo."

I hold up my hands in surrender as best as I can while trying to stay afloat.

She leans over again, but this time a wave catches the boat up just enough. She wobbles and goes right in the water, headfirst. I lunge for her, my heart stopping at the surprise of seeing her go overboard.

Instantly, she bobs up and takes a breath like she'd been holding it forever. Sheer pain fills her features. "Oliver!" Her hands are pushing through the water. "You. Didn't. Tell. Me—" she uses the back of her hand to move her wet hair out of her eyes. "It. Was. This. Cold." The last word was a shriek and her hand slaps the water so that I get sprayed in the face.

"I did!" I breathe heavily, my body's natural reaction to warm itself. My teeth are chattering. I don't remember it being this cold when I was a kid. Suddenly I'm rethinking Sebastian's brilliant idea to build a resort here. Who in their right mind would ever want to visit here and come within a mile of the forsaken, watery tundra?

"I didn't. Think. I was being. Unsafe." She pauses, a shiver going through her entire body. "I'm sorry." Deep breath and a shake. "...about the bracelet. It was. Just at. My feet the whole time."

Yes. I'm an idiot and now we're going to drown following the paralysis of our limbs.

"Let's get back in." I motion to the boat.

"And ruin." Her breathing is labored. "Your nice seats?"

Except, even though her face and skin are pink and her breathing is shallow, she's smiling. I don't think I've ever seen a more beautiful sight. Forget

Capri's lemon trees. Sophie's wet hair, matted and crazy, her eye makeup smeared…that's what fills me up. Unbidden, my arm reaches around her at the waist. I can't help myself from protecting her. She shudders and moves closer to me, her body trembling and her gaze never leaving mine.

I tighten my grip around her waist. The cold is fading, all the reasons I can't pursue a relationship with her a distant memory.

Then, without a word, she takes a deep breath, goes under, and breaks away, swimming away from me. She resurfaces several feet away and freestyles in the direction of the shore. If I don't hurry, she'll leave me bobbing along, alone.

If I don't get my act together, I'll lose her forever. I cannot let that happen. I will not lose Sophie Lawson.

Chapter 11

Sophie

Well, at least if I die here in this lake, the last thing I see will be Oliver. The only semblance of life or warmth I feel at this moment is where his arm was around my waist. As I swim to shore, I think of how his touch burned me there. This is unchartered territory—he's never held me so tightly around my waist before. He's never held me anywhere so tightly before.

I was glad I'd packed a responsible lunch of soup and salad today instead of that giant cinnamon roll that was tempting me. Claire went to a boutique bakery in town and left one out for me this morning. But like an actual adult, I took the nutritious option instead. If I'd had a cinnamon roll food baby, it would have sunk me like a stone for sure.

I shudder at the memory of his arm around my waist, saving me, branding me. I guess I'm glad I avoided the cinnamon roll baby since his fingers and palms spanned my middle so...intimately.

And if we'd gotten any closer, we might have kissed. Which, in reality, was probably less of a possibility, the more I think of it. We were freezing to death.

I reach the shore, and I get the sudden urge to do that thing they do in movies where there's a shipwreck and the character swims to a deserted island for safety. They claw their way through the sand and then turn over on their back, heaving breaths and crying tears of gratitude that they survived.

Except, I'm now out of the water, on all fours in the sand, and my dress is twisted up around my rib cage. In nothing but my underwear, my booty is on fully display. I panic and jam the dress down over my hips again. The fabric is so water-logged, it takes longer to fix than is at all acceptable.

I half wish I had drowned in the drink, as Oliver called it. Then I would have been certain he didn't just see my rear end as I tried to peel the dress down and away from my skin.

Why had I worn this today? I'd been doing so well at wearing the most unsexy clothing I could find. But it's almost laundry day and my pickings were getting slim. Besides, the county council had scheduled a quarterly drop in at the mobile library, and I wanted to look more professional than I had in yesterday's sweat suit.

As soon as I'm as decent as can be expected, I stand and turn around to find Oliver. I don't see him anywhere, and the panic I felt at being mostly naked is nothing compared to the alarm inside of me now.

Where is he? How long has he been under water?

"Oliver!"

I take a couple of steps into the water, getting to where it hits my knees, before he rises to the surface a few yards in front of me and takes a big breath. He must have been doing one of those underwater glides like he's in the summer Olympics. I notice a rope from the boat in one of his hands and it moves along behind him.

"You're almost there, Oliver," I encourage, guilt at putting us in this predicament pawing at my insides. If I'd only better checked the bottom of the boat! In my defense, though, he was trigger happy.

I check my dress again to make sure I'm decent. Even though it's sticking to my skin as if it's been coated in nail glue and I'm one large nail bed, I think I'm adequately covered. He reaches the shore, heaving the boat up onto the sandbar.

I kneel down beside him, taking a second to look at his bare upper half—chiseled, taut skin—before he opens his eyes and my gaze skitters away.

"Are you okay?" he asks, his skin just starting to turn back to its normal color.

"I should be asking you that question."

"I'm good." He's breathing heavily and I can't help but watch the precision and gorgeousness that is his torso as his chest and abdomen work in sync. "It's like I'm Wim Hoff. I've never felt so alive." He grins, lifts his arms, and places his hands behind his head, his breath rate slowing down.

"Vim who?"

He chuckles, his gaze taking me in, pausing a moment at the dress that now feels two sizes too small. "Wim Hoff. That Dutch guy who promotes Arctic plunges. He says they give a state of euphoria like a high from a drug. Lots of people do it." He drops his hands.

Huh. I could see that maybe being a possibility. The cold water did shock me into a state of energy. I shift my position so that I'm leaning on my hand

and have my legs together and curled up on the other side. I glance at the sky, willing the sun to dry me off more quickly. I feel so exposed.

The strange thing is, I don't exactly mind it. Being exposed and vulnerable. Maybe there is something to the idea that Arctic plunges give you clarity. Or make you crazy stupid. Who knows right now? Because my mind is going random, unholy places, dwelling on thoughts of Oliver. I don't care about all the reasons he and I can never be together. I don't care that he'll be moving back to Capri, or that he's not the settling down type.

All I care about is feeling his warmth on my skin. Finally tasting his lips. To heck with the fact that we both have lake water on us. Longdale Lake's known for being crystal clean, right?

And that's when I know that the Dutch guy, Vlim Shoff, Wim Hoff, or whoever he is, knows what he's talking about. I don't care anymore about all the reasons why I've told myself no, where Oliver is concerned. I have more clarity than I have in years and the truth is, I want Oliver. Not just his lips to claim mine here on this beach that is, let's face it, rocky, weedy, and a bit smelly. Warm Hawaiian white sand this is not. But I want Oliver in my life for good. I want him to stay here in Longdale. I don't want him to go back to Capri.

He sits up, too. I glance down and a piece of my hair, still wet, falls in front of my eyes. He reaches up to brush it off my face, pinning it behind one ear. My skin tingles at his touch. His fingertips pulse more warmth into my body than any amount of sunlight could.

All the rest of me—except for the area above my ear that he just touched—breaks out in goosebumps again and I shiver, the electric current between us giving me erratic bursts of giddiness.

"You're cold," Oliver states quietly, his eyes glancing over me with care. He scoots closer to me, wrapping me up in his arms. He sits cross-legged. "Here just lie your head down in my lap and then I'll put my arm like this." I do it, and he lays his arm along the length of mine, rubbing my skin gently.

"Thanks," I whisper, and I'm seized with more violent tremors. Come on, body. Warm up!

"Oh, man," he says. "We might need to do something more extreme. You're freezing." His gaze rakes over me, his eyes hooded. "I think it's medically pertinent that we get out of these wet things and get really close, skin to skin."

I snort, remembering a scene from one of my favorite guilty pleasures. "Like in the third book of the *Twilight* series when Bella and Jacob have to have skin-to-skin contact?" I look up at him, breathing in the concern on his face.

"It saved her life, didn't it? And maybe the lives of countless others who read the book. I consider it a Public Service Announcement."

"In your dreams." I make a squawking sound. "It's probably sixty degrees out," I say. "I'm not going to die."

"Hey, it could save you from a great deal of discomfort. For medical purposes only." He holds up his palms, his facial expression wreaking of feigned innocence.

I push on his chest and move to sit up. "You're so immature. I get now what your mom must have gone through with your childhood antics."

He swallows hard and just stares. Unfortunately, my reference to his mom and his childhood did nothing to distract me from other, more forbidden thoughts.

I want Oliver in my life now, and in a much deeper way than ever before.

"Okay, our clothing can stay where it is." But he tugs me closer, and I hear him whisper under his breath something like, "That *would* be a dream."

"What did you say?" I ask.

He gazes at me. "Nothing, Sophie." And he settles into the sand a bit more, only moving to dislodge a couple of rocks underneath him.

I face away from him and scoot back until I'm against his chest. He rubs my arms, bringing life back into them. We sit like that for a long while, watching the three black ibis dig in the sand only a few yards away.

We should probably get back in the boat now and return to the resort, but I can't bring myself to suggest it. My back up against his chest is life right now.

There's no need to talk about anything at all. We just sit. Waiting for what's left of the sunlight to dry us out. Waiting for me to have courage.

For what, I do not know.

Finally, half my body is tingly, and I move to stand.

I pull him up with me, and we're face to face. His gaze pours over me, filled with so much that I can't understand.

That Wim Hoff thing might be wearing off because my head starts to pound dully. Except it doesn't take with it the insane notion that Oliver and I could be together for real. Not the pretend thing at closing night. But something deep and honest.

I don't want to go back to my safe hamster ball. I want to live in this feeling.

"I can't believe you fell in," he whispers in my hair.

"Neither can I." Embarrassment colors my laugh. "I guess it's only fair. You'd polar plunged without me—for no reason it turned out—I guess karma came around in a swift way."

"Where's your bracelet now?"

A giggle bursts out of me. "I have no idea."

He shakes his head. "I have to admit, I don't care about it anymore."

"You shouldn't. It's probably from Walmart." I tilt my head back so I can better see him.

He scrunches up his nose, and I laugh. Then he grows serious. He tugs my waist closer to him again. His expression dares me to kiss him.

Chapter 12

Oliver

I'm going to kiss Sophie Lawson.

Something close to rage fills me.

No. It's not rage. I'm not angry about it, it's just the pent-up, dissociated feelings of roughly seventeen years of loving her and being too dumb to notice.

I'm claiming her hips with my hands. I'm on a mission and I'm mad that it's taken me so long to wake up to it. I glance down at her mouth and wonder what it will be like.

My brain zips down a dangerous memory lane: I saw her when she was getting out of the water and her dress was hiked way up. But I couldn't disrespect her by lingering. So, I dunked back in the water and found the painter so I could guide the boat to shore.

It was a good thing she'd righted her dress by the time I came back up. I don't want her to feel embarrassed, which she would if she knew what I saw.

But the memory of that will forever be etched in my brain somewhere in the file labeled "Wonders of the World, or How I Discovered the Mind-bending Beauty of Sophie Lawson."

I focus on her face, her lips. The smudge of mascara only adds to the heady heat of this moment. Her eyes track mine, back and forth. I bring my fingers gently around the back of her neck.

Thoughts of Sebastian intrude, and I stop for a second, a flare of triumph burning inside of me.

Hold up. No. I am *not* thinking of my brother at a time like this. And this isn't about one-upping him. I have a gorgeous, funny, intriguing woman in my arms, on a beach, and we're both still moderately wet from our swim that, frankly, made me feel more alive and more comfortable in my God-given manliness than I ever have in my life.

And she seems like she wants to kiss me too, if her shudder just now is to be believed. I never would do this without her full consent, because what if she didn't actually want to and then I go and screw up a perfectly fine friendship?

Crap. What if she actually doesn't want to?

Get your head in the game, Oliver. Go in for the kill and kiss her already. If she didn't want to, she wouldn't be looking at you like that.

I rub my thumb gently across her lips. They're so soft.

"Oliver?" Her voice is a whisper.

Forget Sebastian. Forget her grandfather who would love to write his name in my blood. Forget that low life Troy who used to kiss her.

I stutter over thoughts of Troy, the man who didn't value her and now real anger is starting to course through me. How could he have not valued Sophie? Where does he get off?

Why, oh why on God's green earth am I in my head right now?

Do this now, Oliver.

Before I can mentally wipe these aggravating and inopportune thoughts away, Sophie's eyes close. But it's not the eye closing that happens right before a kiss. Her head's not tilted towards me anymore. She's squeezing her eyes shut. Tightly. As if she's...embarrassed? Upset?

No. No. No. No. No.

Her eyes fly open. "Are you moving to Capri?" she asks, her brow in a harsh line.

"I—" Not what I expected her to say, and I stammer, not sure how to say it, but knowing she deserves the truth. "I have to—"

Her gaze travels over mine. She closes her eyes again and gives one swift nod.

"Sophie," is all I can think to say, my mind begging to go back in time.

I try to pull her close to me again, try to bandage up the chasm that's suddenly between us.

It doesn't work.

Chapter 13

Oliver

I drop my hands and Sophie takes a step back from me, her bare foot sinking in the sand. She jams one hand against her lower back and the other one to her forehead, like she's annoyed and checking for a fever.

"That was..." She shakes her head and wets her lips, her gaze to the sand.

"I'm sorry." I don't know what I'm sorry about except for everything. For spending years being like Troy and not seeing her worth, at least not clearly enough. For missing our standing date last year without more notice or thought for her feelings. For not kissing her. For almost kissing her.

Her cheeks burn red, and she gives a laugh that's hollow. "What are you sorry for?" Her lower lip trembles, but her voice is strong and she turns away, placing both hands on her cheeks. "It was just...I don't know. A momentary craziness?"

She nods at her words, and my stomach grows sick.

"A momentary craziness," she says again. "And I'm sorry, too. Not that either of us should be sorry. Because it was nothing." She guffaws. "We should not be sorry for nothing," she says definitively. She whirls back around and aims her pointer fingers at me. "Should we head back? Before Sebastian sics the dogs on us?"

Sebastian doesn't have dogs. But I'd much rather stick to non-existent dogs than to the subject of what almost happened. What I wanted with my whole being to happen.

"Speaking of dogs, how's Wilford?" I ask, relieved I could bring up a safer topic.

She gives me one last look of sadness…regret…before her features change to a mask. She latches onto the idea of Wilford and we run with it, talking about him the whole way back. I've never had a dog as an adult because I'm never in one place long enough, but if I ever got one, Wilford would tick off most of my boxes. Except, I don't know how I'd cope with the massive amounts of hair he'd leave in my Mercedes.

My arms and shoulders burn from the rowing, but it's good to get out my aggression. I welcome the pain because this kind is a lot better than if I allowed myself to think of missed opportunities.

As we near the dock, I see the resort in its finery and feel a surge of pride. It's nearly ready. It's an homage to Longdale Lake. I realize that in some ways, it's an homage to our childhood as brothers, and to Sophie herself.

Now I've gotten all nostalgic and sentimental. Which isn't acceptable.

I can't do this. It's a good thing we didn't kiss.

With that sour thought, I help Sophie off the boat and her hair is almost dry. She's somehow cleaned off the makeup smudges under her eyes.

We begin walking back to the resort. The moment we had is now char-broiled to a crisp between us. I could try to salvage something. I'm not going to try to kiss her—I can't do that to either of us. But I could do something friend related...or boss related.

She reaches down to pick up the shoes she'd kicked off in our earlier escape, and I find mine, too. The bush it landed in is only a little worse for wear.

"Want a milkshake? I owe you one from last August."

Her brows rise and then fall. She continues to walk. "Can I take a raincheck? I'm a little sick to my stomach. Seasick. Besides, Shake, Shake, Shake isn't open for the season yet." She sighs. "I think I'll just go home for the night and work on the purchasing tomorrow."

"I'm sorry you're not feeling well." It's my fault. I'm the one who roped her into going out on the lake without even asking her if she wanted to. "You go home and rest. And promise me you'll let me buy you a large black licorice peanut butter cup one soon."

"Will do." She nods once and picks up the pace. "I just need to run up to your office and get that printout I left yesterday."

I don't want her to leave on this awkward note, but I'm grasping at straws and coming up empty handed.

We walk across the terrace and to the back doors. They don't slide open, though.

"Locked," I tell her as I try, and fail, to open them. "Let's go around the front." I'd rather do that than text Sebastian and ask him to help me. He's still angry that I ran from him, guaranteed.

We circle around the premises, following stone steps and pathways in silence. Her steps are long and purposeful, but without warning, she stops short. Her entire being goes stock still.

"What is it?" I ask, alarm settling over my skin.

Her gaze is steely, arching out past the grounds of the resort and beyond our property to the beach. A couple of fishermen are walking in our direction. They don't seem to have noticed us.

"Hey, that's that guy. Mr. Wallis?" I ask her. I narrow my eyes. "And that must be his son. Your..."

"Ex. Yes." She finger combs her hair and starts walking again.

Troy the Ex lifts the hand holding a fishing pole in something of a wave. "Sophie?" he shouts. He doesn't sound happy to see her. Even though they're

still several yards away, I can feel the tension emanating from both Troy and his dad.

Sophie lifts a hand, her smile plastic. "Nice to see you," she shouts in a friendly way. It's dismissive, and I'm relieved we aren't stopping to chat. Neither of us glance back over to them as our pace increases, and once we're inside the front doors and into the lobby, the smell of fresh paint stinging my nose, I resign myself to the fact that she's leaving for the night.

We reach the elevator doors, and she jams her thumb into the button, pushing it three times for good measure. We don't say anything until the door bings open.

"I gotta say, I'm speechless here." I don't know whether to try to think of something nice to say about Troy the Ex, or if I should state the obvious. I choose obvious. "Soph." I shake my head and whistle. "He's just...not what I pictured for you."

She grunts a snort laugh and folds her arms tightly. She's quiet as we wait for the elevator doors to open.

When they do, she pushes past me and I have to speed up to catch her, her shoes tapping on the tile floors. "What did you expect him to be like, huh? A cover model for some cologne body spray?"

"Well, I didn't expect him to look like he belongs on the cover of *Fish and Stream* magazine."

She shoots daggers from her eyes as we reach my office door. "Oliver." Her voice is a low growl.

"Okay, sorry. It's really strange seeing the guy you almost had kids with."

She stops short, her chest heaving with deep breaths, and then continues on ahead of me. We walk in my office, and she snatches up the printout. "I didn't almost have kids with Troy," she shouts. "We never set a date and he never gave me a ring." She shrugs, but it's overexaggerated. "Get over it! He was a decent guy who was kind and took me out every Friday night to the Presidio and he was fine with Wilford, so—"

"The Presidio?" I repeat. I roll my eyes. "Every Friday? Did you go at four so you could be sure to eat with all the retirees celebrating their Golden anniversaries? Come on, Soph, you're meant for more excitement than that."

Her jaw is set at what looks like a painful angle. She swallows. "Life isn't just about excitement, Oliver. You're such a...a thrill seeker that you don't take time to smell the roses. My life here is good."

I don't exactly know what my point is, just that I want her to understand one thing.

"You deserve a lot better. That's all." I throw my hands up and feel stupid for the way my voice cracked at the end. "And being 'fine' with Wilford is not acceptable. That boy is a beast and a rockstar and you deserve someone who appreciates him as much as you do."

Her lips twitch, but she glares at me again. "You don't know what you're talking about."

Now I've really done it. I've ticked her off, and I haven't even said what I wanted to say, which is: *I want to be the better man you deserve.*

I shake my head. "You're right. I don't know what I'm talking about," I say. "I want you to do what makes you truly happy, that's all."

Her eyes are like fire. "I don't need you telling me what I can and can't do, or what does or doesn't make me happy. You have no right, Oliver."

"Exactly, I have no right," I agree. "But maybe I want to have a right somehow. I've wasted so much time and I—" I take a step forward. I wish we could pick up where we left off on the far shore.

"I'm sorry, Soph. I'm realizing things that I should have realized long ago. And I can't go back in time, but it doesn't hurt to try to make up for what was lost, right? I mean, I'm here now and I think you're an incredible woman..." I trail off.

"You're leaving Longdale in a few months." Her voice is sharp.

"Don't you ever want to go sometimes? Even just for a year or so? You don't have to stay here forever." Sometimes I wonder why anyone could want to stay here long term.

"I know that, Oliver. This is my choice. I—" There's something in her eyes, like the defensiveness in her tone might be more to convince herself than me. She presses out a palm. "I'm not leaving and you're not staying. So? What then? What is there to discuss?"

"I could probably come back here, though, after Capri is up and running," I offer, but at that thought, my chest clamps shut. I don't want to live in Longdale. Sometimes the fresh, clear air here feels suffocating. I can't explain it, but it's real.

"Probably?" She shakes her head. "You should see your face right now. You look like you swallowed something bitter." She starts to pace. "I would never ask you to do something you find so difficult."

She gives me a worn smile, then pushes past me. When she reaches the door and goes to turn the knob, she whips back around. I brace myself, because it seems like she's going to yell. But she just looks at me, like she's trying to assemble all the fractured parts of me into a recognizable whole.

"There's a staff bonfire on the beach tomorrow night. Will you come with me?" I ask.

Her mouth moves without sound before she says. "I don't know."

"It's up to you. It starts at eight and I wasn't planning on going because…" I shrug. "Because it would bug Sebastian more if I didn't. But now that you're an official freelancer employee person, I can invite you."

"Maybe." She turns the doorknob.

"If you decide to come, it's going to be over by the dock. You know, through the tree canopy."

"If I can come, I'll look for the big fire on the beach. That should clue me in on where to go." She leaves, closing the door soundly.

The whiff of passive aggression from her that I used to find so funny feels different now that it's directed at me.

The past half hour was terrible. I was an unthinking idiot.

But at least I finally opened my mouth and started the conversation. To what end, I don't know. Probably nothing.

At least I said something, and she didn't run screaming from my office. Was she happy when she left? Absolutely not. But she didn't run screaming.

I feel like I'm the guy from the movie *Dumb and Dumber*. *So, you're saying there's a chance!*

I've opened a door. It might be one of those tiny, rounded hobbit doors, leading to a fantasy land that goes nowhere. But at least it's open now. And all I know is, I don't want to ever do anything again to make it close.

Chapter 14

Sophie

What was that?

Oliver! The nerve of that man. He has played with my heart long enough. Does he realize what he does?

I'm really, really, really glad we didn't kiss.

Except. What was he saying about wasted time and that I'm incredible?

I'm walking to my car and texting Claire wildly. I don't care about the typos as my fingers fly over my phone.

Strange moment with Oliver just now. Things were so good on the boate and then we ended up in the water but things were still good and he miht have wanted to kiss me and I might have let him but then he just stood there with this vacant look on his face and I don't know I think he paniked and then Troy of all peple shows up and I felt nothing it was weird like I never even had a relationship with him at all and then Oliver started saying something about making up for lost tume an...

I curse as I accidentally hit send too early. I walk the rest of the way to my car. I should probably sit down to text out something as monumental as this.

It takes less than a minute for Claire to call. I'm feeling vulnerable from my stream-of-consciousness text. "City administrator jobs totally rock," I say. "You can get off at five and be at my beck and call whenever I need."

She ignores my opening. "Your run-on sentence should win an award." Claire's voice holds worry. "And, are you okay? I don't think you've ever misspelled 'might' before." There's a pause. "Or the word 'people' or the word—"

I interrupt. "I don't know if I'm okay." I put the phone on speaker and slump down in my driver's seat. "I should probably come home before I have a freaking trauma response to what just happened."

"Trauma response? Start from the beginning. Why were you on a boat with Oliver? And it capsized? What in the heck?"

"It didn't capsize. There's a reason I smell like fish and it's not because we went out for seafood." I sigh and start my car. I wasn't kidding about the trauma response. "I'll explain everything when I get home."

"Are you okay to drive? Sisters don't let sisters drive in a funk."

I assure her that I'm fine. I'm hoping I'll make it home in one piece, as the strange points of interest in the dumpster fire that is my life replay in my mind over and over.

When I get there, Claire already has a long, thin rice bag warmed up for me. My dumpster fire-ness must have come across over the phone.

Wilford gives me tons of kisses, liking the way my skin tastes now that I have dried lake water on me.

Claire eyes my crazy, seaweed-like hair. "You really did go overboard."

I nod, but then rush to explain. "It was near the shore. The far shore. We were trying to ditch Sebastian, and—"

"Who would ever want to ditch Sebastian?" It's a reflex of hers. Sebastian's this hot, surly beast, prowling in a castle. Completely unattainable, but a lot of women around here don't ever want to stop trying.

I laugh as I remember the scene. "I don't know exactly why Oliver was trying to avoid him, but we had so much fun. And then he jumped in the water for me, and everything was like it was in slow motion, you know? And then we reached the shore, and I wanted to kiss him on the beach."

Claire holds up a palm. "Wait. You shared a romantic moment?"

"It was..." I stop, not even sure I want to try to explain it to her. Doubts rush into me. What even was that? "I don't know exactly. We didn't kiss. But we almost did. And then I asked him if he was going to move to Capri and he said that he has to." The pit in my stomach grows. "But then later, after we got back to the resort and saw Troy and his father in the distance, Oliver was super agitated. And he started talking about wasted time and how I'm an incredible woman."

Claire's eyes grow wide. "He said that? You mean there's a Tate brother who actually notices other people?"

My heart sinks to my stomach. "You don't have to do that."

"Do what?"

"Villainize someone just because they might be interested in me." Wilford has settled his huge head on my lap. I knead the hot rice bag hanging from my neck and finally, there's some heat seeping into the bones of my fingers.

Claire opens her mouth to protest, but then her gaze goes to the floor. "I'm not villainizing him."

At my tongue click, she holds up her palms. "I admit it, I never liked Troy and made that clear to you from day one. But that was because I knew he wasn't right for you. So yeah, I villainized *him*." Claire grabs her hair, sweeps it to one side and holds a section of the ends close to her face, probably looking for split ends. It's a habit I caught myself doing just this morning.

"And what's so wrong with Oliver? He's nothing like Troy," I shoot back.

Claire drops her hands and lowers herself on the love seat across from me. Since Wilford usually picks me over her, I get the sofa. Wilford's ample body needs a whole lot of room. "It's—you guys have always been good together. I think, fundamentally, he's a good guy who could make you happy—" She works her jaw. "—If he'd ever slow down enough to invest in a relationship. Frankly, I'm surprised that now, after all this time, he's showing interest. I wonder why. I wonder what's taken him so long. If he sees you as just another fling...if he were to hurt you..."

My heart pounds in my ears. She's voicing the very concerns I used to have. "I get it. He's unpredictable. And when he touched my face—Claire, he touched my mouth." Even now, I can feel his thumb brush against my lips, feather light, stoking every nerve ending in my lips to ignition.

Claire's features have softened. "So, he went in for the kiss and then you asked him if he really was going to move away?" she asks quietly. "You guys need to talk."

"I tried, but I didn't know what to think about what happened. And then we saw Troy, and Oliver was just so...territorial."

Claire jumps up from the love seat and walks to me. She kneels down and rubs Wilford under his neck. "He was territorial, like a dog? Troy made Oliver jealous. That's so crazy that it—"

The thrill of it all hits me again. "What? Claire, he had to wait until I'd met and broken up with Troy to realize his feelings? It's just so maddening. He's too late."

"Maybe he's finally opened his clueless, lazy eyes," Claire says with a grin.

"Lazy eyes?" I laugh. "I don't think that means what you think it means."

She throws her head back in laughter. After she composes herself, she grows serious. "It looks like it's in your hands, Sophie. Do you want him or not?"

Her question jolts me with the same sharp surprise of a bee sting. "You know I do." I attack the rice bag with a massaging fury. "But he'll never stay put in Longdale. We discussed that too. He's not staying and I'm not leaving."

Claire tilts her head from side to side. "Well, you live half the year here, and half the year who-knows-where?"

"The council would really love that. 'Hey, I'll run the library for half the year, and for the other half, you guys are on your own.'"

"Or you could design resort libraries full-time?"

That thought feels exciting and daring. Terrifying and purposeful. I'm not ready to give it wings, though.

My breaths are ragged. This conversation with Claire doesn't solve anything. He's still a nebulous entity, readying himself to fly away in a matter of months. But if the opportunity to kiss him were to present itself again, I might.

I love the man.

Claire leans in for a quick hug, then carefully removes the rice bag from my violent hands. "You should probably go shower," she says gently. She gives me this look like I've been in a coma for months and can't be trusted with anything. Which may be more true than I'd realized, seeing as how I'm in such a daze, I could have walked right in the shower with the rice bag around my neck, completely ruining it.

She watches me so carefully that I know she's concerned. I don't want to deal with that right now. I need to get the aroma of Longdale Lake off me, so what if Wilford is fascinated by it?

After the shower, and after Wilford processes that I don't smell like fish anymore, he lumbers onto the bed with me. It's my mom's bed, the same one I climbed in when I had a bad dream when I was little. He maneuvers and squeezes into his favorite spot: right in the middle.

"I just need to stick with you, Willie Boy," I say, burying my head into the softness of his neck.

He sniffs me again and heaves a gentle sigh. I doubt Wilford can understand me, but even still, I adore my dog.

I *should* just stick with my Wilford Babe.

Chapter 15

Sophie

The next day, I'm running late and I'm all kinds of mad about it. I woke up with my head still thick from lake water and Oliver. I love the man, okay? But he's leaving. Part of me wishes I could leave Longdale, too. Actually, that part is growing by the minute. My promise to my mom to take care of Claire, and my ties to my mom and Longdale because it represents her, feel muddy now.

Instead of Longdale being my safe cocoon, it's starting to feel like it's squeezing me a little too tight.

I drive over to Tollark, a town about five miles south of Longdale. It's Violet's day off, and I'm late opening up Scott. And yes, even though I'm only a few minutes late, it bothers me. A lot of things bother me. The stacks, with those chipped shelves that sag in the middle, make me want to write a nasty letter to whoever from the county denied my bid for a slight budget increase so we could replace them.

Why'd they even have to build this town here anyway? I haven't had a single patron after an hour of me sitting here looking at the blasted, chipped shelves. Even though this means I have plenty of time to dig into the newest Colleen Hoover title, I'm still in a mood about the lack of patronage. Apparently, no one around here likes to read. I bet no one would even notice if I stopped coming.

I check my computer, my stomach growling. Yep, there are only six books due back here today. They were checked out two weeks ago. And I'm not scheduled to leave until two, when I can take my lunch break before driving over to Menton for the three to six p.m. slot.

I'm tempted to leave early, though. I should just make a big sign and put it up on the Food Mart's door. "Attention all you non-literary minded people. I've gone home for the day. Maybe I'll come back in a year when you all decide you want to stop wasting my freaking time."

Irritated at the childishness of my own irritation, I clank down the metal ramp, in need of some fresh air. It's a mostly empty parking lot and it's April in Colorado, which means cloudy skies. But the air is crisp and clean.

"Sophie, I'm glad to see you, dear." It's Oliver's Aunt Stella. I find myself glancing around to see if he's here, too.

That would be a big, fat "no."

She pulls me into a hug that feels like a combo of my mom and my junior high body pillow.

"What are you doing in Tollark today?" I ask.

She unzips her purse. "I like grocery shopping here," she says, pointing to the Food Mart. "They have a much better bulk foods section than our store has." She pulls out a shopping list.

She's not wrong and I guess since she's retired from teaching school, she has more time to drive a few miles for some bulk flaxseed.

"How's the mobile library today?" But from her tone of voice and the way she sizes me up, I can tell she already knows I'm feeling ragey.

"You know, it's been really slow." I wave my hand over the bus. I swallow down the sadness. "But hopefully we can get some patrons to come out today."

Stella eyes the sky. "It's the perfect day for reading, with these clouds." She gazes at me, "I hope you get more people in. How about I come and see what you've got today?"

We head inside the bus and suddenly, maybe for the first time ever, I don't feel like talking about books at all. I feel like talking about Oliver.

She beats me to it. "I was happy to hear you're helping the boys with their resort library. They need your expertise."

I slump down into my seat at the desk up front. "I'm excited to choose a good collection for them."

The impossibly tight quarters of the bus allow for one marginally comfortable reading chair. It's near mine and I motion for her to sit.

She shakes her head. "I'll look at the books first." She puts her purse down on the chair and steps over to the stacks. "You know, the boys have really changed over the years." She's not looking at me, just at the books, running an index finger over the spines. "I wonder who's going to be the first to settle down. Once one does, it will give the others permission to, as well."

"I don't think the Tates will ever settle down. At least not all of them."

She clicks her tongue. "They are ambitious and stubborn. And they don't know what's best for them. The whole lot of them." She turns to me, her blue eyes soft. "But they're good people. Their hearts are gold. When's Oliver going to take you out on another date?"

I know I thought I wanted to talk about him, but now that she's brought him up, I'm not sure I can. "Another date? We've never even been on one date before, Stella."

She stares me down. "What do you call the third Saturday in August? Sophie, that boy has been dating you longer than anyone."

Whoa. That's...unexpected. "First of all, he's not a boy. He's thirty-three years old." I smile.

"You're right. He's a grown man, yes. But compared to my age, he's still very young."

"And second of all, those weren't dates," I say. "He dates actresses and CEOs of companies and, who knows who else."

"There's a difference between them and you, Sophie."

I harrumph a very unladylike sound. "Yeah, I know." Instead of blurting out all the ways those women are better than me, I think it silently.

She cocks her head to one side. "Sophie. I've seen him around other women, those women he's taken out on dates. Not that he's ever brought anyone here, or to Denver. But I do travel with my brother and his wife sometimes to visit their kids. So I've met some of his women friends."

"I don't need to hear about them." I roll my eyes. I hate feeling like I'm sixteen again, when jealousies were so hard to drop.

"I don't want to talk about them, either. The truth is, though, they seemed to be wonderful women. But the spark wasn't there." She draws back, her gaze daring me to make the inference she won't boldly state.

Can people just say what they mean? Can't people just be direct? I know I'm not. And I want to be. I think breaking up with Troy and telling his father I won't chair Longdale Days was a good start.

But I know that Stella isn't the type to interfere in the love lives of "the boys." She prides herself on that, on letting them just *be*. It's one of her best characteristics. Where their parents push and pull them to success, Stella is the non-judgmental relative to fall back on.

I'm in a salty mood, so I don't want to run with what she's saying. I don't want to give her a wink and a "I know what you mean" and then be happy that I just might have a chance with him.

"Stella, he's moving to Capri soon."

"Not *that* soon," she counters. "There's plenty of time to explore the possibilities."

I shake my head. "And then what? A very long, long-distance relationship?"

"I think going to Capri with him sounds lovely."

Swallowing, I want to argue that point, but I can't. "There's this obligation I feel to stay here. There's Claire, and the house, and my mom's grave..."

"Those are all important things..." She trails off.

She only quirks half a smile as if to say, *But if you want it bad enough...*

"He doesn't want to settle down," I counter. "He's talked about not having any evidence that relationships don't have to end in misery."

"Defensive tactics to protect himself. Not that they're unfounded, of course. Thomas and Celine have had a rough go of it, and their boys have suffered." Stella nods, her face weary. "My sweet Charles." She places a hand at her throat. "If we hadn't lost him far too young, the Tate boys would have seen what a healthy marriage can look like. As it was, they'd stay with me when their parents were having particularly rocky times. It's heartbreaking, when you think of it. They had fun with me here in Longdale, but for some of the boys, it put a bad taste in their mouth. Their parents would argue and ship them here. It was hard."

"I thought Thomas and Celine traveled all summer for business."

Stella's mouth twists to one side. "It became that way, yes. But the first several summers? I took the boys to give their parents some space to work things out."

Was that one reason why Oliver couldn't stand the thought of building a life here with her? Did Longdale have ghosts of his family's pain imbedded within it?

"Regardless, I see the way he looks at you," Stella says. "He might need permission from you, though, Sophie. You two have shut each other down so much over the years, it's become a bad habit. This might be stating the obvious, but why would he come back here on the same day every year for just a friend? You're not just a friend to Oliver." She shrugs and begins pulling random books off the shelves.

A flame of hope rises in me. "I think I'm beginning to understand that now."

What if I could see what's really going on? It's like when your brain sends thoughts down the little rivulets in your grey matter, passageways that become like well-worn ruts in a dirt road. We think things automatically because that's the easiest route to take. And yes, I know this because I read a book about it. No surprise there.

Can Sophie and Oliver be more, though?

I'm thinking of myself in the third person and that's kind of odd. But maybe that's okay.

Maybe Sophie and Oliver have a sliver of hope after all. Is there a chapter in Longdale's story that is titled "Soliver"? Or maybe "Oliphie"?

I cringe at our terrible couple name possibilities, and realize that I've never allowed myself to make one up before. Even if they're terrible, maybe the fact that I can go there right now is significant somehow.

It's not until Stella slaps an armful of books down on my Formica desk, cluttered with an old computer, that I dare look her in the eye. She looks down pointedly at the books. And that's when I giggle at the absurdity of the titles she's chosen, and it all assimilates like lined-up toy soldiers in my mind.

Falling for your Best Friend by Emma St. Clair

Brave New World by Aldous Huxley

Maybe Someday by Colleen Hoover

A Long Time Coming by Megan Quinn

The Pursuit of Love by Nancy Mitford

Stella, you old devil, you. How could I have ever called you subtle?

Chapter 16

Oliver

I'm overeager, standing on the beach with Tate's Longdale Lake Resort's thirty or so employees and their families, waiting for Sophie to come like I'm five years old, dying to open my presents at Chuck E. Cheeses.

All day, my office was a sauna, my pants were a vise around my waist. Whatever it was that I ate for lunch—I can't for the life of me remember—didn't sit right. All in all, it was a beautiful day in the neighborhood.

But I'm here at the bonfire now, the cool night air calming me a little. I even managed to play some beach volleyball and frisbee.

Sebastian gives his speech, ninety seconds long. He only did it because Britta told him he had to. The food is brought out and gobbled up. Our chef, Lionel, the only guy we trust to execute our resort restaurant openings, has provided some casual food, like deep-fat-fried cauliflower (which is delicious and tastes nothing like cauliflower) and pigs in a blanket with a smokey fry sauce dip. Perfect bonfire food.

Except Sophie doesn't come. I'm trying to regroup. I stare into the flames, and roll up the sleeves of my green, flannel shirt. A couple of the groundskeeping staff members have their guitars out and the air smells like smoke and water.

Nine o'clock rolls around, and people are starting to leave. I ache to see Sophie.

I pull my phone out of my pocket to see if I can manage texting her without coming off as a hoverer.

"You're on your phone on a night like this?" It's Sophie, standing in front of me, her back to the fire and silhouetted by the glow behind her. As she moves closer to me and sits on one of the logs next to mine, I see she's wearing flip flops, cut-off jeans, and an oversized, Longdale High sweatshirt with a hood.

"I was texting you to see if you needed a ride over here."

"Well, I'm here." She gazes into the fire. I do a double take at the way the glow from the flames highlights and shadows the curves of her face.

"You missed Sebastian's speech, but there's some food left." I stand to walk over to the food table, my heart pounding. She made it.

She follows me and I hand her a paper plate. She grabs some pigs in a blanket and squirts mustard on her plate.

We sit back down on the stumpy logs, but she only takes a couple of bites. She sets her plate on the sand. "I'm not that hungry right now."

Most of the employees and their guests have already left, and I introduce her to those sitting near us. Unsurprisingly, she already knows half of them—the half who are local to Longdale. I turn back to her. "Did you eat before you came?"

She shakes her head and pulls a piece of hair away from her face. The wind has picked up a little, so maybe it's a good thing the bonfire is starting to die down. We sit in silence. I wait until the rest of the people leave.

When it's just Sophie and me left, I ask her what I've been wanting to ask her ever since she got here. "Are you alright, Soph?"

"Claire and I went to Mom's grave."

Her mom died before I knew Sophie, so I don't know a lot about her. Sophie's been tight lipped about her, and I haven't wanted to push.

Until now. I mean, I don't want to push her to say more than she wants to. But I want to know. I want to know everything.

"That must have been hard," I offer.

She pins me with a look, but her voice comes out soft. "No, it wasn't hard. She's been gone for twenty-four years." The shake of her head dismisses me. "I barely remember her."

Except there's sadness cloaking Sophie and if it had been the old days, when we were just friends, I would have shoulder bumped her and then tried to make her laugh.

But now, things have changed. And I'm not sure what to do. Seeing the pain in her eyes makes my chest thrum. I have to help somehow. I know I can't fix this, but I have to try.

"Is Claire doing okay?"

She nods, pulling her sleeves over her wrists to cover her hands. I wait a long time before speaking again.

"My parents spent six straight months away from home once," I say. "I think they came back for a couple of days. But even then, they weren't at the house much, just sort of in the vicinity. Work was everything to my dad. And my dad was everything to my mom." I stare into the fire. "My stomach hurt the entire six months. Stella came out to Denver to be with us for part of the time, but she was teaching and couldn't be there long. We had supervision, our former nanny came and stayed with us. But it was like my parents didn't exist anymore. Or that we didn't exist to our parents."

I reach for her, pulling her into a side hug.

"I guess what I'm trying to say by telling you this is I know how it feels, on a much smaller scale, to be abandoned by your parents," I say. "It's not the same as what you've been through, not even close. But I'm here if you ever want to talk about it. I'd love to just listen."

Even though she's wearing a sweatshirt, her back and the back part of her arms must be cold. Because as hot as a spring campfire in Colorado is on your front, the cold night air can slice like a frozen blade in back.

"I'm sorry about your parents being gone so much." She glances at me, sniffing again.

"And I'm sorry you lost your mom." I bring my other arm around and envelop her more deeply in my arms. At first, she stiffens, and I wonder if it's because of me, or because she just went to her mom's grave and has her walls up.

After several seconds, I decide to end the hug. I won't be that guy who makes everything uncomfortable or doesn't read the signals she's laying down. But just as I start to pull away, her log wobbles and pitches her forward in my arms.

"Whoa," she says.

I catch her. I steady her forearms and we stand. She wraps me in a hug.

It's unlike any hug I've ever had. Because it's Sophie and her breath tingles across my neck. And the fronts of both of our sweatshirts are warm, but now that we're super close, our bodies sink into each other. Her hair smells like fresh peaches.

And now I'm craving peaches. I'm craving Sophie.

"I lied," she says.

"You don't lie."

She snickers against my chest. "Oliver, everyone lies. Some a little, some a lot. But everyone lies."

I chuckle. "Okay. What did you lie about?"

She breathes in deeply and lets it go in a rush. "I do miss my mom. Visiting her grave is hard. And I hardly ever do it, which makes me a bad daughter, especially because her gravestone was dirty and the grass had started to grow over the edges. And I'm a bad sister because Claire likes to go."

"You're a good sister to Claire."

She shakes her head. "There's something else I wasn't honest about. I do remember her. Memories fade, but I remember lots of things about her. It still hurts that she died." Her voice is raw. "I'm still so angry about it."

"Anyone would be." I pause, and when she doesn't say more, I add, "Anytime you want to talk about your mom or anytime you need anything, I'm here for you. Okay? I haven't been there for you in the past, but I want to be now." I swallow down the regret. Some of it starts to shift and free itself, out and away from my chest.

She softens into my embrace, inching closer so that her legs are practically flush with mine. She tilts her head up to me.

I care for her so much. Her pain brings me pain. All these years with her have completely changed me. I realize with startling clarity that she's my best friend—she always has been—and I'm in love with my beautiful, tantalizing best friend. I don't know the future, but that doesn't matter. My eyes ask a question, and she nods.

Breathless, I press my lips to hers. At first, I tease her with my mouth. I'm not kissing her softly, there's no way I could do that right now. But there's some caution there. She's on her tiptoes and she stumbles as she tries to push herself more firmly against me.

Now we're feverish. Hungry. I've never known anything like this before. Her lips are hot, searching. They taste like vanilla lip gloss. Pulling me closer, her hands splay my back, and I don't want this to end.

I need her closer to me, so my hands move up her shoulders and into her hair. I tilt her head the slightest bit, my lips traveling to her neck. A low moan vibrates in her throat, and I ache to move back to her mouth.

Suddenly, a soft, wet, dog nose presses against my arm.

Chapter 17

Sophie

"Down, boy," I mutter against Oliver's lips, moving my knee against Wilford.

Oliver's lips. Whoa. Wow.

And now he's roaming, and I like it.

But then he pulls away, and with a flushed face, he asks. "Do you mean me or Wilford?" His voice is low, dangerously low, and his forehead is pressed against mine.

He knows I meant Wilford, but his expression is challenging me. Questioning if it's okay or not.

I bend to pick up Wilford's leash. How he broke away from the sign post I tied him to, I don't know. It's probably because I was so anxious to find Oliver, I wasn't careful with the knot.

I wind the leash around my arm and lean in for another kiss. My pulse thunders through me to my fingers and toes. After a few moments, I break apart, my breathing uneven and rough. "What do you think?" Now my voice is low and froggy. A lump I can't swallow is in the way. Wilford seems much happier now that we're a foot apart.

Oliver's eyes widen. He crushes me with another kiss. It's just me and him and the heat of the bonfire. Nothing else exists. His lips move with mine. Everything's in sync, and with our bodies flush against each other, even our heartbeat's the same.

Just as Wilford buries his nose at our hips to separate us, someone clears their throat. It's subtle, but a definite warning.

Oliver pulls away, and his eyes over my head are like daggers. "Sebastian, do you mind?" He pulls me tighter up against him and goes in for another kiss. But suddenly I'm shy. I move away, just slightly, but Oliver feels it, and he tightens his hands against my back before letting me go.

He scowls and I begin to understand. He thinks I've pulled away because of Sebastian.

No. It's time once and for all to let Oliver know that he's the one.

He's the one. It's always been him.

That's when I grab his shirt, my knuckles jamming into his hard chest. A sound of surprise rumbles deep in his throat as he continues to kiss me, and I find myself matching his groan. I'm vaguely aware of footsteps trudging away in the sand. Good. Maybe Sebastian's given up and will leave us alone.

After a moment, we both need some air. We're panting and Oliver's cheeks have gone a shade of warm red.

My head bows and I grab the hem of my sweatshirt. I can't match his gaze. It's too much. The heat from the bonfire, the heat from the kiss, I can no longer tell which is which.

My gaze catches on a blob of mustard on my sweatshirt.

Seriously? All these years spent wondering what Oliver's lips feel like and I've gone and kissed him while wearing a ratty, old sweatshirt that I spilled mustard on?

Oliver barely even glances down at the mustard stain in the shape of the African continent. He frowns again. "Was this—? Are you okay?"

I nod, a ball still in my throat.

"Do you want this, Sophie?" His expression is pained.

"Does a bear want honey?" I half giggle, half inhale. I let go of my sweatshirt and cover my mouth with both hands.

He smiles. "I want this, too. I didn't know how to figure—us—out." Now he's gesturing between us.

"Right. Right." I'm nodding. "I know. I'm not sure, either."

He tugs me closer. "Side note…" He brushes his lips across the top of my forehead, ending in a small kiss just above my eyebrow.

Above my eyebrow? I never knew a kiss there could affect my whole body.

"If you ever *don't* want me to kiss you, don't wear this sweatshirt, okay? Because it's amazing on you."

I laugh again, but realize he's serious as he's staring at me, his gaze boring into me. Oliver's sultry eyes are a sight to behold. I wish I could tell my sixteen-year-old self: *Don't worry, Sophie, in the distant future, he'll be giving you the look of a thousand knights in shining armor. Just you wait.*

He circles his hands around my hips, breathing in my hair. "You smell like fresh peaches. I love your shampoo." He inhales against my head. "How do you smell like peaches and not campfire right now?"

I take a step back. "Thanks." I chew on my bottom lip. "True confession? I'm wearing doggy dry shampoo. Juicy peach scented doggy dry shampoo."

The shame. The shame!

He tips his head back and laughs. He looks at me and shakes his head. "I love that. Does Wilford know you borrow his beauty products?"

I shrug and feel the corners of my mouth twitch. I've only had to use it twice, ever, and both days, I ended up spending time with Oliver. "I ran out of mine, and his was almost brand new. It works." I dip my head to the side like I'm about to do two air guns and shoot him with a wink. Thankfully I stop myself before I get too far into *that*.

We're standing here, downright sloppy silly grins on our faces, when there's a gigantic slosh, the sound of water pinging against metal. Suddenly the bonfire is out, hissing with steam. Sebastian and one of the employees of the resort are standing there holding a large metal can. "Let's pack up and go," Sebastian barks.

Oliver starts to cough because of the plumes of smoke emanating from what's left of the bonfire. I feel a tickle in the back of my throat and begin to cough, too.

"You could have warned us," Oliver says to his brother, looking like he wants to shred him to bits. I pick up my paper plate. At some point, Wilford scarfed down what was left of my food.

Oliver grabs my hand, and we walk further away from the smoke. The temperature is dropping with the fire out. My hands and feet are ice. Or maybe that's just my shock response from Oliver's kisses.

Maybe smoke follows beauty, or kissing couples, because it's following us, and Wilford is rearing up and barking at it like it's alive and going to attack.

"Wilford, it's okay." I crouch down to calm him, and see the mustard stain again. My first instinct is frustration at spilling. But Oliver likes me in this sweatshirt. He said if I didn't want him to kiss me again to be sure I didn't wear it.

We actually kissed.

I wrap my arms around Wilford, marveling at the wonder of it.

"It's gotten cold so fast," Oliver says.

"We should probably head back." I stand, and Wilford jumps up and barks again, threatened by the big, scary whisps of smoke. His leash rips away from my hands and I wince. "Ow!"

Oliver is quick to respond, stepping to Wilford and grabbing his leash before he makes a break for it. Wilford is six years old, but he still acts like a petulant puppy.

"Are you alright? Did that hurt your hand?" His brows jam together, and he gently lifts it to his face. "I don't see any signs of rope burn, but..."

"I think I might live," I offer weakly, not able to stop my teasing smile.

He chuckles. "With a couple months of treatment, you might pull through?"

"Maybe. If you're lucky."

"If I'm lucky?" His gaze darkens. "I would be lucky if I'm by your side."

He slings his arm around me as we walk to the terrace, through the resort, and out the front.

By his side? The phrase reminds me that our time together is short.

We reach my car.

"Sophie, I just…" He stops himself and instead brings my hand up to his lips. The brush of a kiss on them leaves them white hot and I wish he would do the same to my mouth. Again.

He feels it, too, I think, because he does that low grumbly growly thing in his throat a second time. "I just want to say that I'm glad I'm back here in Longdale with you."

I've watched enough RomComs to know how this works—that saying goodbye for the night is such sweet torture. Except in a RomCom, there would be a light rain, and there wouldn't be a dog whimpering nearby.

"I'm glad you're here, too," I say as I open the back door of my Corolla, get Wilford inside, and close the door. He whines and paws at the window.

"Aw, he wants me to ride with you guys." Oliver places his hands on the glass over Wilford's paws and I want to die over the cuteness of it.

"Thanks for inviting me," I say.

"Thanks for coming." His expression grows serious.

I get in my car and before I can close the door, Oliver leans down and gives me another kiss, this one soft and slow.

I feel the dog squeeze his head through to the front.

"Wilford!" Oliver yanks his mouth away and slaps a hand over his cheek. "His tongue is huge." He wipes his face.

I start to laugh and shove Wilford back onto the rear seat. "I'm sorry," I say to Oliver.

"It's okay." He reaches past me and gives Wilford a good scrub under his chin. "He's just feeling lonely, aren't ya?" Oliver's sweetness to Wilford is threatening to make me melt even more, so I insert my key in the ignition. I've got to get out of here fast.

As I leave the parking lot, I check him out in the rearview mirror, and he's staring after me. My heart hurts with longing. I glance over at my glove compartment. Only I know what it contains, and now, the little secret object is like a talisman that has finally brought Oliver to me.

I drive home and stumble after Wilford up the front steps and into the house, drunk on kissing. Drunk on *love*.

Chapter 18

Oliver

The next evening, Sophie comes to my office after working at the county library during the day.

"Hi," I say, leaning against the door frame, my hands in my pockets. For some reason, I feel a little shy.

"Hi," she says back. Her smile is barely there, but all her emotions are in her eyes. She seems to be feeling a lot like I'm feeling: happy, a little cautious, and maybe a lot in awe of the events at the bonfire.

I didn't sleep much last night, wanting to relive the kiss and solve all our problems. I want to figure out a way we can be together, in the same town, and both still have everything else that we need. By the morning, when I forced myself out of bed, I knew I still didn't have any answers. I just didn't seem to care because I wanted to see her--bad.

Now, Sophie's working at a small table near the door, and I can't keep my eyes off her. I can't sit still, either, so I'm pacing around the room, trying to sort out in my mind some work issues.

She's filling out an online book expense form for the accounting department.

"Hey, so Soph?" I finally ask.

"Mmm hmm?" She answers, her eyes trained on her screen.

"Did I tell you what Sebastian said?" I'm looking out the window at the lake, still pacing.

One beat of silence, and then she says no.

"I told him you needed an office," I say. "And since he's so stingy with the square footage, he suggested I carve out some space in here for you."

I feel her glance over at me before turning back to the list she's making, but she doesn't say anything, so I reroute my pacing to face her.

She's wearing jeans with holes slashed through the thighs and knees, and an oversized t-shirt that says, "I have no shelf control." It has a graphic of a messy, overstuffed bookshelf. I don't know where she got it, but it's perfect for her. Her hair is braided to one side. I want to kiss her again.

Sophie levels her head at me, her gaze steely. "Sounds good." So much passes between us in a second—hope with an underside of caution. At least I hope I'm reading her correctly. I know that's how I'm feeling.

I nod. "Good. Consider this your office, as well." I spread my arms wide. "What's mine is yours."

The corners of her lips creep up in the smallest of smiles and then she turns back to her work.

I sit down at my desk, pick up my phone, and text Britta, Sebastian's personal assistant: *Operation: Sophie's Desk is a GO.* Except I can't stay seated anymore because I'm excited all over again. I get up to wander around my office some more.

In less than thirty minutes, we have delivery people from all over the county and even Denver bringing items in. Britta, who is sort of a bossy grandmother type, comes by to grin at me before I covertly shoo her away. She rolls her eyes, much like she did this morning when I was explaining my plan in an animated way. Once the delivery people get going, I manage to stay seated at my desk for a whole ten minutes.

At first, Sophie barely pays them any attention. But pretty soon, it's hard not to. Especially when the technicians from an interior design firm in Denver come in and literally start applying temporary wallpaper above where she's sitting.

She pushes her chair out and walks over to me. My body is buzzing with an acute awareness of her every move. I try to play it cool, pretending I'm too wrapped up in my work to know she's standing by my desk.

She puts her hand on her waist and tilts her head, sticking out her bottom lip subtly. "So...what's this?"

I fight the urge to gush, *I can't live without you Sophie and I need to show you that, so I'm shamelessly buying your affections and showering you with a cool workspace.*

"I wanted to create a little area here for you. Give you your own space," I say instead.

Her eyes are big as she points. "A French-style blonde carved desk with a wash of white paint?" She sits and spins around. "The fanciest desk chair I've ever seen that happens to be—" she bounces twice on the seat. "—uncommonly comfortable. And now a—" She tilts her head to the side to look more closely at the wall covering I'd chosen. "Bright blue wallpaper with birds on it?"

"Remember your French obsession?" I chuckle as I think of the summer between our junior and senior years after she'd had two semesters of French. She kept spouting off random words in the best accent she could manage and started collecting anything that reminded her of a place she didn't think she'd ever visit. She still hasn't.

"Thankfully I never went so far as to wear a beret." She shudders and then smiles. "Beret wearers, man. Gotta love 'em."

"Exactly. When I saw these pieces, they reminded me of that. The wallpaper company said this would look nice with the desk."

"It looks spectacular." Her gaze takes everything in before returning to mine, her surprised expression melting into something softer. "Thank you." She moves closer to me.

"I wanted to make it special for you." My nerves shuttle up through my stomach and into my chest. I'm putting myself out there, and it's equal parts exhilarating and terrifying.

She reaches in to give me a swift kiss. Someone from the office supply store in Granger comes to set up one of those little gold organizers filled with pens, pencils, and paper clips. "I'm glad I get to hang out with you." She touches my shoulder and I meld into her touch.

Almost before I can see the openness in her gaze, she clears her throat and turns to grab her laptop. "Okay, here's about thirty titles I've chosen so far." She sets the computer on my desk and leans in, her perfume filling my head.

I look at the screen but, embarrassingly, I'm unable to pay attention for too long without filling my head with everything Sophie. I'm irritated that the wallpaperers are still here. I should ask them to step outside so we can have a moment to ourselves.

"So, we have the classics, Shakespeare, Faulkner, Allende and so on." She points to a book site's cart. "I thought it would be nice to have those in leather bound editions, so they last a long time. But I added some current popular pieces, and then some complete collections, like the "Harry Potter" series. I thought we could have a small picture book section, since some of your guests will have kids."

"I like it when you talk literary to me."

Her gaze skitters, and she clears her throat again. Her tongue flicks her lips before continuing, her forehead lined with a scowl. "Then there's the matter of where to put them all."

I need to slow the flirting for now. And figure out a way to help her maximize the embarrassingly tight space we've given her.

"It's more visually appealing to have the books spread out on the shelves," she says. "To have some forward facing and to put little decorative items on the shelves. You don't want this massive block of books with titles you can barely read."

"You don't?"

She clicks her tongue. "No. You haven't visited Scott lately, have you?"

I hadn't and I regret it. There are so many things I regret.

"Can I come over there soon?" I ask.

She stares at me before nodding. "I'd love for you to come." My heart starts beating faster at her nearness. She turns back to her computer screen. "The thing I'd love to try is sort of the same way a bookstore displays their books. You want to make everything visually appealing. And if we had more space, we could even provide a sitting area for kids, too. Maybe a small set of table and chairs...and a bean bag..."

She frowns as she trails off and I know she's realizing there's no room for that. This resort library thing was just supposed to be one little amenity. Sebastian never meant to hire a consultant.

But Sophie's vision has gotten a hold of me, and I want her to dream bigger, like those resort libraries she showed me online. I don't want Tate International's to be small and weak. And I've done her wrong by not pushing Sebastian more on this.

I've done her wrong in a lot of ways over the years.

I plan to rectify that, if she'll let me.

"Hey, Carpets Plus is here." I point as two men carry in a rolled-up rug on their shoulders. It's plush and the lightest shade of pink they had. I want her to be able to slip her shoes off and enjoy it.

Her mouth drops open. "You got me a rug?"

"Of course." I want to trace the curve of her cheek, but I shouldn't do that type of thing at work. I also resist the desire to thread my fingers through the hair at her scalp. "I want you to be comfortable."

The carpet people have laid the rug down. She slips her shoes off even before she reaches it. "Ooooh. Yeah. Oh yeah. This is *alright*." She smiles at me, and her nerves and cautiousness melt away. Her gaze is raw and filled with desire.

Yes. Yes, it is alright. It's all good. I just have to figure out how to either find a way to stay here in Longdale with Sophie from now on, or, better yet, convince her, somehow, to come to Capri with me.

Chapter 19

Oliver

I'm at a book show in Denver with Sophie and it's the best time I've ever had.

Don't tell my brothers this. They'd take offense that a book show is more exciting than our Swedish cruise last year where we saw the Northern Lights while eating calamari. But it is.

Book shows? Huh. I didn't even know they existed.

Turns out they're like a mix between a tradeshow, bookstore and Comic Con, complete with nerds dressed up in literary character costumes and where authors are treated like celebrities getting high on praise from their massive fans.

I don't know whether to walk around shushing all the librarians or go get in line and gush over some writer's book signing.

Sophie's in heaven. This is her element—her Super Bowl of the librarian world. She's hugging people like they're long-lost relatives, and I don't think it's exactly necessary to point this out, but Sophie's by far the most beautiful librarian in the bunch. And there are a lot of librarians here.

It was a week ago that we kissed on the beach, the glow of the bonfire nothing compared to what I was feeling in my chest. Sophie's kissing is something else. It's a surprise wrapped up in your favorite t-shirt. Or sweatshirt to be exact, because she looked unbelievable that night.

Now, she's in professional librarian clothes: a dark green blazer and skirt. I admit I'm excited by anything she wears.

We've been together every evening since the bonfire, hanging out at my place or hers until the most sensible thinking one—usually that's Sophie—insists we call it a night. Saying goodbye is stupidly hard.

"Sophie from Marshall County!" Another fifty-something woman screams while giving her a hug.

Sophie greets her by name. I'm pushing one of those smaller metal carts behind her, like the ones they use at the grocery store for when you are going in for just a couple ingredients for dinner. Except this thing is heavy with books because Sophie's been running around like a kid on a sugar high, fussing over the binding of the book before she smells them. Of course, she smells them all as her eyelids drop closed. I've never seen anything so attractive.

I've got it bad. The thing is, what we have hasn't been defined. We're both avoiding conversations of the future or what this means. I'm not thinking about having to return to Italy.

Staring at Sophie is more fun than thinking about leaving, so that's what I do instead. I've caught myself staring at her multiple times today, and

I'm pretty sure she's caught me a few times, too. The thing is, the way her neck curves to meet her hairline is something to behold. I don't get to see that part of her very often because her dark, wavy hair covers it up. I have to wait until she stops to look at something at a table. She leans over and palms her hair to one side so it doesn't get in her way. That's the moment. It's mesmerizing and I can't stop looking at her in case I miss the next time.

After our second time through all the booths, we take a break in a quiet corner of the convention center. "I'm completely out of money," she says. She pats the towering stack that I'm finding increasingly difficult to push around.

"It's the library's money, right?"

"Yes. I get an allowance from the county and normally just order the books online. But once a year, I get to do this—" She spins her finger around to take in the conference center. "Did I tell you this one isn't even out yet?" She paws through several hardcovers until she finds the right one. "And they're only selling a limited number. Mary from the Shelley County Library told me they're already out of them." She presses the book to her chest and hugs it close. "I'm fortunate."

"I think I'm the fortunate one." I tug her close and realize the book is stuck in between us. It's too bad, but it will have to do. I place a small kiss on her forehead, and she draws back, her gaze searching mine.

"What do we have here?" She glances down at my mouth and then back up to my eyes.

"I don't exactly know what we have...just what I hope to have...if you'll have it..." My tongue is thick.

"That's a lot of haves." She smirks.

I let go of her with one hand to scratch the back of my neck. "That's because sometimes it's hard to find the words when I'm around you."

She bites her bottom lip, sets the book on top of the stack, and tries to push the cart forward. It's heavier than she thought it was, so the inertia of her body slams into the stationary cart, sending the towering stack flying.

We scramble to pick up the books. "You haven't even broken a sweat pushing this thing around." She kicks one of the wheels with her Vans slip-ons. "My books are gonna break this thing and you're not stopping me from adding more."

I finish restacking, hoping none of the pages are creased. "I couldn't stop you. That would have been cruel. Besides, the people of Marshall County need these books."

She offers a small smile and starts to push the cart again. It's slow, but she's doing it. I know her enough to know not to take over. "You've got it. Just push with your legs," I say.

As we round a corner, I place my hand on the small of her back and the other one on the handle to help steer. "The turns are the worst," I mutter, glancing at her.

Her lips thin out and she grits her teeth. "I should have waited until one of those dollies was available." She's managed to straighten the cart and we're walking towards the exit to pay for everything.

"Does this happen every year?" I ask, my hand still next to hers.

A smile curls her mouth to one side. "No." A couple of steps later, "Yes. But I think I deserve it for the many hours I spend dealing with Scott."

"You do deserve it."

"So, about what I said earlier," I venture.

She looks at me with brows raised. She darts her tongue out to wet her lips and flips her hair back.

She looks behind her and that blessed, beautiful back of her neck is a neon sign that I can't get over.

"I've loved this past week," I try, my heart pummeling my rib cage. "And it seems like maybe you have, too?" Except at that last word, my voice cracks. I feel a zip of embarrassment and suddenly, I'm back in the shake shop again, trying and failing to get my game on.

"It's been really—" she swallows, her gaze going to me before continuing on ahead, "—really great."

"It has been. I hope things work out, long term…"

Her sharp intake of breath stops me from going further, but then the corners of her mouth curve into a small smile. "We care about each other. That's good enough for now."

It has to be, but the thought of this ending, whether because I have to move away again or any of the other reasons stacked against me, is impossible.

Someway, somehow, I have to figure out a way to never say goodbye to her again.

Chapter 20

Sophie

I've finished prepping my new books and they're nearly ready to be put on Scott's shelves. I've savored the job, sealing the binding tag with a firm hand. It's one of my favorite things to do at work.

I stand from my desk and step to the stacks. Now for the hard part: choosing which books to remove in order to make room for these. The new kids on the block are here and my old babies are going to need to step it up to show me whose time has come.

The computer can tell me that. It's a simple algorithm: years on the shelf divided by number of total checkouts and boom, the ones with the highest scores are gone. Either to a storage closet at city hall until it's time for them to reappear, or to be sold. Except it's not that simple, because there are certain books I just can't get rid of.

That's kind of like Oliver, come to think of it. The algorithm in my brain tells me things with him will never work out. I'm small-town Sophie, and Oliver hates small towns except if they're located in Italy and end in the letter I.

Or maybe he just hates Longdale?

In any case, I have this urge to ditch the algorithm and go with my gut instead. He's like those books that in theory don't make the cut, but I just can't quite part with them.

Not that he doesn't make the cut because he's somehow deficient. Oh boy, no. He's everything. I thought that I loved him for all those years. But what's happening now? My soul is on fire and set free. What I feel for him is more than I could have comprehended before.

But he said something about long term, and I froze up. I constructed the thickest hamster ball I've ever experienced, which is frustrating. I just want to be free to love this man.

Except, the way he pronounces the name of Capri should have given me a hint of the divide that exists between us. He says it with the emphasis on the "Ca," and I say it like "CaPREE" like Capri Sun drink pouches, which let's face it are delicious and I sometimes still put one in my lunch.

I have freaking Capri Suns in my lunch and Oliver has lunch brought to him in fancy packaging by Sebastian's assistant, a hipster named Drake.

I laugh to myself. Stranger things have happened than two opposites getting together. And instead of obsessing over questions of the future, I can try to live in the now.

I shift my focus on the books, ready to wrestle an older non-fiction home décor title from the stack's clutches, when a family comes into the library.

Three little kids, plus the mom and dad. I've seen them here quite a bit, and I swoon over the cuteness of a family reading together.

I'm so focused on them that I don't notice someone else is in the library until I smack right into the bouquet in a glass vase they're holding. Its roses, daisies, and mums are scratching my face and arms as I try to spring back and away from it.

Did Oliver just bring me flowers, and did I just ruin them?

I fall down hard on my rump, on account of the stack of books in my arms. Falling down in a mobile library ain't pretty. The whole thing pitches and sways like the vessel in *20,000 Leagues Under the Sea* when it gets rammed by the mysterious green monster.

Everyone rushes to my aid, which also is not pretty since the walkway is not a two-lane highway and I've got three adults trying to help me up. Totally nice of them. But I realize then, once the enormous bouquet is out of the way, that it's actually not Oliver who is holding it.

When I'm upright again, the guy with a flower shop uniform hands the flowers to me. "Sophie Lawson?" he asks and I nod, a little dizzy.

I know instantly they're from Oliver, and as much as I could die from the heady gloriousness of the scent and intricate beauty of the mix—these are some high-quality flowers—I struggle to find somewhere to put them.

Again, I'm freaking out about the metaphors here. This enormous bouquet just does not fit in the mobile library. There's not a single flat surface big enough to accommodate it. It's like Oliver. Oliver himself is too big and exciting and smells way too nice to fit into my life.

A thin throb begins forming behind my eye while I head outside to stow the flowers near the ramp. A niggle of truth scratches at me: Oliver is to me like a vintage wine is to a juice pouch.

I rip open the card:

Thinking of you. This bouquet's beauty is nothing compared to yours. Love, Oliver

I giggle and smack my forehead. When my heart begins to skitter, I rub my breastbone.

Is this real life?

Somehow, I'm able to focus on work, and a few hours later, I drive Scott back to Longdale and park him in the county offices parking lot. I open the back seat of my car and brush away as much Wilford hair as I can. The flowers should improve the smell in here. Wilford—gotta love him—leaves a distinct scent wherever he goes.

I shut my car door, the squeak from my Corolla's ancientness reverberating through the air.

I drive away, out of town, and onto Lakeside Road heading to Longdale Lake and the resort.

Oliver knows me. He knows this is where I belong, and he's still kissing me and sending me flowers. He designed an office space for me, and he pushed a cart full of books around the book show like he was my groupie bodyguard and I was a celebrity.

I didn't miss the look in his eyes that day. He's into me.

When I pull up to the resort, I almost forget to even put the car in park before getting out to rush up to see him.

Chapter 21

Oliver

I'm in my office, waiting for Sophie, and putting off work. My stomach contains a kaleidoscope of butterflies, which is something she told me once—that a group of butterflies is called a kaleidoscope.

I can't wait to see her. But I'm also thinking of this morning, when Sebastian mentioned something in a meeting with finance about the billable hours for freelancers being higher than expected. He had the nerve to give me a dirty look.

I reminded him that I used my personal funds for the office décor, and that Sophie's job is only temporary. Yes, his all-seeing eye promptly found out about the mini makeover I did.

Are there rules against dating freelancers? If I were to ask our mom, she'd probably say yes, but then smile and ask me who I was interested in and how serious it was. I wouldn't ask Dad—but if I did, he'd tell me I should have been married three years ago, but that dating anyone connected with the company was a bad idea for our public image.

I get exactly nothing productive done until Sophie arrives, and after chatting with her for a few minutes, my head has cleared. I think I can finally focus on work.

Now if I could stop glancing over at her every three minutes.

"What would you think about this write-up for the resort website?" Sophie asks, not looking over at me. A new email from her comes through.

"Normally, I'd ask our copywriters in Denver to do this." I glance over the short paragraph describing the resort library, smiling at words like 'cozy yet sophisticated.' "But it looks like they won't have to earn their keep on this because it's brilliant."

I think of my attempt at a "Define the Relationship" talk the other day at the book show. That wasn't really the time or place for a discussion like that, so I don't blame her for shutting it down. She did acknowledge that we care about each other and that's enough for now.

I hope it is. My return to Capri is always there, though, at the back of my mind. It pulses into my awareness. I want to invite her to come with me—maybe that will be the right move soon. I know she's the poster child for all things Longdale. But a stay in Capri wouldn't be permanent. She might love to get away for awhile.

I come to myself as she pipes up again.

"Thanks for saying that. And thanks for the flowers." She stands from her desk, walks over to mine, and holds out her hand.

I take it and stand. "I hope they were as pretty as the website promised."

She puts the hand not holding mine over her heart. "Oh. They are divine. Finally got the dog smell out of my car."

"Wilford." I laugh and shake my head.

"They did almost kill me, though."

"What almost killed you?" I'm laughing because Sophie's dramatic. Things are life and death much of the time.

"The flowers."

"You're not allergic to flowers, are you?" I suddenly realize there's actually a lot about Sophie that I don't know. Which reminds me that I didn't value her like I should have, didn't pay her the kind of attention she deserved. I won't make the same mistake again.

She laughs. "No, I'm not allergic. I think you'd know if I were."

I want to know. I want to know everything about her.

"But it was so big," she continues. "And I hadn't heard the delivery guy come in, so I turned around, ran right into the bouquet, and fell." She smacks her forehead.

"Oh, no." I gather her in my arms, my hands low on her waist.

She rolls her eyes. "I'm fine. My rear end is a little sore."

Any mention of any number of her body parts will have me distracted and I can't let myself go there right now.

"I wish I could have delivered them myself, but you know," I say. "The grand opening is coming up, and there's a lot to do. This is crunch time." The loads and loads of to-dos keep getting longer by the minute and I feel the pressure of needing to get this right. So what if this is our tenth property? This one's extra special. And I realize, with another zing across my stomach, that this venture cannot fail. Our Bahamas property? That could have failed, and it wouldn't have been the end of the world.

Yes, it would have been a huge problem, but it wouldn't have impacted Sophie or Longdale.

This time around? I can't stop myself from thinking that if this resort fails, I'll fail Sophie, too.

"Is there anything else I can do that's not library related?" she asks. "I'm still working on contacting some of the local authors we'd like to feature, but I can definitely switch gears if needed."

"Soph, I'm alright. But how are you? For real?"

Her mouth opens and closes, and she leans back to take in my expression. "For real? I'm a little confused."

"I'm not sure how to do this," I say.

She gestures between us. "This? You're doing this quite well." A smile teases her lips. "But what about in a few months, when you tell me you're dating some Mediterranean woman you meet in Capri?"

She pulls her fist in front of her mouth.

"No. It won't happen. I don't want to date anyone else. I want to date you."

"But you *are* leaving."

The ball in my throat is growing. "You're right," I say, my gaze a deadlock on hers. "I'll be leaving when my agreement with Sebastian has been met. That's how this has always worked. That doesn't mean things can't change after that."

Her brows shoot down, her gaze laced with disbelief. "You don't want to run off to another adventure?"

"I don't think I do."

"But what about Capri?"

"I still have to go. There are a lot of moving parts. I need to schedule a trip soon." I scratch the back of my neck. Thinking of those moving parts weighs me down, like for the first time, I'm dreading going back and having to face them.

A shadow crosses her face, and my thoughts grow desperate, trying and failing to grab ahold of anything that might help. "But I don't want to stay in Capri long-term. I want to come back here with you."

She searches my gaze. "There's a reason you've never stayed here in Longdale for very long. It's Longdale. You would die a slow death of boredom."

"Before? Maybe. Now...I don't think so." The town *is* growing on me, maybe because I'm seeing it through Sophie-colored glasses.

"I—as much as I want that to be true, you can't know for sure how you're going to feel after you've stayed here for awhile—" Her face holds strain, her eyes tired.

I nod. "I'm not sure how it's going to work." I level my gaze at her. "But I know what I want."

"Do you, Oliver?" She puts her hands on the sides of her head. "This is all so new."

"It is, but it isn't. I've known you for a long time, Sophie."

She looks down at the floor. When she doesn't respond, I feel pressure in my chest. "What do *you* want?" I ask, my throat hot.

Her eyes grow wide. "I don't know how to answer that."

"It's a simple question. What do you want?" My voice is rougher than I'd intended and so I take a deep breath before continuing. "I'm falling for you, Sophie, but I'm not sure how you feel about me."

She eases in closer to me. At first her scowl has grown and even though I worry because it means she's not happy, it's just so attractive that I kind of like it.

Then the scowl softens, but her expression is still intense. "Come with me," she whispers, and grabs my hand.

I don't care where she's taking me. I'll follow her anywhere.

Chapter 22

Sophie

I'm still holding his hand, my arm stretched out behind me as I charge down the hall, into the elevator, where I don't meet his gaze, and over to the main entrance. I hope he can't hear how loudly my heart is beating. It's like the tell-tale heart, ratcheting louder and louder the closer we get to my car.

It's nearly dark, and the air is crisp, almost cold, but I'm hit again with how beautiful the area surrounding the lake is.

We near my Corolla and that's when I start to second guess myself. I'm not sure if I can do this. Is it too late to go back to the office? Maybe I could just ask him to fix the gas cap or something. It hasn't been closing tight lately.

Or maybe I can suggest we get in the back seat and make out? My stomach drops to my feet at that thought, but then I realize there are probably security cameras out here.

So that idea is pretty much out.

No. I summon my resolve. Oliver's asking how I feel? He's gonna get how I feel, once and for all.

I open the passenger side door and lean over so I can open the glovebox.

"The ritual of making out in one's car is traditionally carried out in the backseat, but whatever..." he says.

I straighten just in time to see the shrug of his shoulders, a wicked smile playing me.

"You are just..." I smile, shaking my head. I have no idea how to finish that sentence. I don't mention that I was just thinking about kissing as well. Still, my head grows warm.

Clutching the silver spoon behind my back, I lean against the open car door frame.

Am I ready for this level of vulnerability? It's a risk I didn't think I'd ever have the opportunity to take and now that it's here, my thoughts and feelings are everywhere.

I take a deep breath. "You keep saying you don't know how I feel about you and it's true, I haven't been very good at showing you. It's hard to put into words. I get tongue tied and then I start going on and on and..." I stop myself and clear my throat.

I pull out the spoon from behind my back and hold it up in the air. Waiting, I say nothing.

"It's a long spoon." Oliver nods and gives a nervous smile. "Okay! And you keep it in your car because...?"

I flip it over and show him the engraving. His eyes widen. He grabs it from me and pulls it closer. "Shake, Shake, Shake. Thirty-year anniversary." He glances at me before studying it again. "Wait. Is it still on here?"

He runs a thumb over the rough spot before he sees it. "I remember this," he says. "I painted this heart on it with your nail polish."

"It used to be bright red, but it's faded."

"I bought this on a whim one night when we were working." His grin stretches wider. "Mostly it was customers buying these commemorative spoons, right? You kept making fun of me about what a waste of money it was." He chuckled. "But then you were waiting for a ride from your grandpa, and you had some nail polish for some reason."

"It was in my purse," I feel a little defensive. "You never know when you're going to get a chip! I was trying to quit chewing on my nails. It worked for awhile." My nervous laugh seems to make him smile. "Anyway, remember? You finally handed it to me when I was painting my nails at a table outside after the shop closed. You said you wanted to give it to me. And then when I wasn't readily accepting of your gift, you grabbed my nail polish—"

"And had to fight you off for a minute because you kept trying to get it back," he says with a laugh.

I massage my forehead at the memory of our antics. "But then you painted a heart on the handle, right here. You blew on it until it dried and that was that."

"You still have it."

"Oliver, this might sound lame, but as soon as I got my own car, I put it in the glovebox." I pause, fighting the fear. "And that's where it always is.

I can't get rid of it. And I guess what I'm trying to say is—my feelings for you are only growing stronger over time. I want this with you."

He leans in closer to me, his gaze intense, and I take in his bounteous, rolling hills of cedar scent.

How can the way he smells be both all-consuming and so subtle that I crave more?

"Sophie," he breathes.

Right as he begins to cup my cheek to draw me in to kiss me, I hear a woman's out-of-breath voice behind him.

"Oliver, I finally found you."

He stiffens in my embrace. The magic is gone.

Chapter 23

Oliver

After recovering from my shock at hearing Miranda Miles's distinctive voice here in Longdale, I realize I have to pull away from Sophie. I so don't want to. And I'm still holding the spoon. It's bent and scratched, but I'm struck with a huge sense of nostalgia and longing.

Miranda is dressed in a black and white business suit that reminds me of something my mother would wear. That makes sense since she's a childhood friend of my mother's. She twists her mouth to one side and glances down at the spoon. Neither Sophie nor I have said anything yet and it's getting a little awkward.

I start gesturing with it. "Miranda? It's good to see you. What brings you to Longdale?"

Sophie takes a step away from me. One hand is kneading her side.

"My assistant didn't call you?" Miranda shudders and groans. "Well, I did fire him shortly after I told him to reach out, so maybe he didn't do it."

If memory served, Miranda had a habit of going through personal assistants like breath mints.

"No. I didn't hear anything from him." I pause. "Is there something I can help you with?"

"I realize this is very late in the workday, but I had a last-minute trip to see my parents in Sacramento, so I thought I'd take a jaunt up here and meet with you in person." She holds up a satchel, which I'm assuming contains real estate stuff.

Real estate stuff. For my residence in Capri.

I turn to Sophie. "Sophie, this is Miranda Miles. She's one of the real estate agents we work with. Miranda, this is Sophie Lawson, a dear friend." I wish I could introduce her as my girlfriend, but we still haven't defined what we have.

Miranda laughs. "One of? My, you like to try to humble me, huh, Oliver?" She extends her hand to shake Sophie's. "Oliver's buying a house in Capri. I've narrowed it down to a couple and need his feedback. Real estate there is extremely competitive and done mostly by word of mouth."

I stammer, my head growing full of heat and confusion. "I asked Miranda to start looking there for me a couple of months ago," I tell Sophie. "She's an expat living in Europe."

Miranda nods, and places a hand on a hip. "It's so exclusive, you can't buy your way into Capri. You have to ease your way in, you know?"

"*If* it ever comes up." I shrug, willing Sophie to understand that things have shifted for me. I can see the wariness in her eyes. "And most people who live there want to pass their property on to a family member rather than sell. You were saying a lot of wanna-be buyers lose interest in the process before they even get anything."

"But not Oliver Tate," Miranda assures. She turns to Sophie, but her gaze keeps going to mine. "I think what makes the Tates so good at business is they are patient."

"Sounds like she knows you guys really well," Sophie says, opening her car door again and placing her bag in the front seat.

"I guess so, but I may have had a change of plans, Miranda—" I start, not sure what I should do, or even what I should think. Things are so tenuous with Sophie.

"I say we order some food and go over all of this tonight," Miranda says.

I glance over at Sophie, wanting more than anything to tell Miranda I can't. "Miranda, why don't we get you set up in a room at the resort for the night. We're not fully operational yet, but we do have some comp rooms." I shift my attention to Sophie, hoping Miranda will take the hint and leave. "Sorry, just a second," I tell Sophie. "I'll ask Sebastian about a room for you before I go home, Miranda. The real estate can wait until business hours tomorrow."

Miranda shakes her head. "But by the time we meet tomorrow and discuss everything, their business day will almost be over. It's in the middle of the night there right now." She yawns and places the back of her hand over her mouth. "I'm exhausted myself. But we have to get a jump on this, so they see your offer first thing."

Before I can respond, I hear Sophie's driver's side door close. She's behind the wheel, and her stiff smile about does me in. She rolls down the Corolla's passenger side window. "I'll see you tomorrow, Oliver. It was nice meeting you, Miranda." And before I can stop her, she's driving away.

This wasn't how things were supposed to go. I was supposed to thank her for saving that spoon and tell her she's my world. Everything else that I thought was my world before just took a backseat.

My insides chill. Miranda made it sound like I've got one foot in the door in Capri—like it's only a few formalities until I have a house there.

A dream I've had for years—of having a house there—tastes like ashes on my tongue now. As excited as I used to be about that prospect, now I only want it if Sophie's there with me.

Chapter 24

Sophie

I'm at my kitchen table, staring at the last three designs I've sketched over and over again. Nothing is turning out quite right. I'm so out of my league here.

I decided to work on the resort library project at home tonight instead of Oliver's fancy set up he made for me.

I want to see him. But when his real estate agent, Miranda, went on and on last night about Oliver wanting a home in Capri...I don't know. It put things in perspective.

I can't ask Oliver to give that up. Despite what he says about wanting to make things work long-term with me.

I've established that I can be on the dramatic side, right? So of course, I went there in my mind...Oliver and me, together forever. But that means he either gives up Capri, and maybe even his job with Tate International, or I give up my life in Longdale.

I can't do that. My whole life is here. As frustrating as the patrons can be sometimes, I love them. I love Scott, antifreeze smell and all. And there's Claire to think about.

I was nine when I promised my mom, as she was dying, that I'd take care of Claire. And I have. We still have the house—we still have each other. And the thought of leaving that all behind feels so wrong, even though sometimes lately, it weighs me down.

I push away the stack designs and get up from the table. Wilford has been begging from me for the last twenty minutes, even though he just ate a bowl full of food. He scoots his generous behind closer to me, a pretty picture of perfect obedience. He's a good boy, but I won't be fooled that he's that good. "I can't feed you vegetable ramen, Wilford," I tell him for the last time, crunching the styrofoam cup into my overly full kitchen garbage can.

My phone rings and I see that it's my grandma. Or it could be my grandpa. They still have their landline, so who knows? Sometimes I hand the phone over to Claire when they call because she's far more adept at managing things. First of all, they're nicer to her. And second of all, she usually lets their criticisms roll off her back much more easily than I do.

I answer the call because Claire's out grocery shopping, which is why we ate cheap ramen. The pickings are slim around these parts.

"Hello?" My stomach rumbles and I wish I had hipster Drake to call up and bring me whatever I wanted.

"Sophie, it's your grandmother." This is how she's begun every phone call I've gotten from her for as long as I can remember. Still as formal as ever.

"I've heard from Lisette Jordan," she says. Lisette is one of the few people my grandma stayed in touch with after they moved back to Boulder once their duty to raise us girls was through. I could even say that Lisette is one of Grandma's closest friends. But even they hug stiffly when they see each other.

"I haven't seen her at the library in awhile. How's she doing?"

"She's concerned."

Uh oh. My throat grows sore.

"She's on several committees for Longdale Days and was telling me that you've not signed up to help any of the committees. That's not like you, Sophie. Is everything alright?"

Let the shame-based games begin!

"Everything's fine. I'm just really busy, Grandma." But I'm not about to explain why I've been busy these days.

"Well, everyone's busy, Sophie. But Longdale Days is coming up and I just don't see how you don't have a minute to spare to help out. At least with the children's art festival or something. You're so good with children."

It could have been a compliment, but the undercurrent means it's not. Usually when she tells me I'm good with children, the surrounding conversation has something to do with the fact that I haven't had any yet.

"I'll reach out to Lisette. I'm sure I can find time for a little job or two." I don't mind helping with something small. I'd been planning on it all along. I've just been gun shy at the thought of talking with anyone about

Longdale Days. I didn't want to end up having to run the entire carnival by the end of the conversation.

I trail my hand along the stack designs I've been creating. If she knew I was freelancing for the Tates, she'd freak.

"She also said something about the resort." Her question-not-a-question hangs between us.

Shoot. Shoot. Shoot. Of course my grandma had heard about me working with the Tates. Why else would she call?

"Well, I was asked to help with the resort library and although it's been problematic for us, it's there and we can't fight it anymore. I figured the least I could do was make sure their library wasn't a complete disgrace." I scrunch up my nose and hold my breath, hoping she'll be satisfied and drop the line of questioning.

"Help with the resort library?" Her voice is filled with disdain. "What kind of flimsy excuse is that? Throw a bunch of books on some shelves. Why do they need you?"

"They want it to be nice. Professional." My voice croaks.

"I don't see how you can even associate with them. They've been trouble since you were a teen."

The wind has been kicked out of me. I massage the back of my neck. "Grandma, that incident with the canoes was totally harmless." Oliver, some coworkers, and I may have borrowed the neighbor's canoes and gone out for a midnight jaunt on the lake the summer before senior year. We may have gotten caught returning them three hours later—unharmed and good as new, I might add. Even the neighbors forgave us, eventually. But my grandparents can't seem to do the same.

"Sophie," Grandma says. "You know how their actions have affected us financially, too. I just hoped you'd have more sense, more courtesy, than to *work* for them."

"They had the winning bid. And I know that was hard." A rush of confusion sweeps over me. I live my life and they live theirs. But if they're still blaming the Tates for their company's struggles, how will they ever feel okay about Oliver and me?

I want a life with him. I don't know what that looks like, but I want it.

"It was more than having the winning bid. That explanation is too simple for such a complex issue, Sophie," she scolds. "They basically pitted the whole town against the turbine plan. We could have gotten more funding, more investors, if they hadn't poisoned people against us."

"What evidence do you have that they badmouthed you or the turbines?" I should stop now. There's no way to win an argument like this. There's almost no chance this conversation will come to any sort of resolution at all. We'll just drop it and pick it up again another time.

"Really? You have to ask that?" Grandma starts to laugh in her breathy way. It's a sound I rarely hear. "It was all over town." She pauses. "That's beside the point, though. The fact is, it's humiliating for us that our granddaughter is working for a family whose actions have cost us a great deal in lost revenue, and a great deal of community respect."

Great. How's she going to feel when she learns their granddaughter is a lot more than just a freelance consultant for Oliver Tate?

I text Oliver later on, while lounging on the sofa, using Wilford as my personal heater. I don't mention the convo with my grandma because I'm still hoping it's just part of their favorite hobby, hating all things Tate, and that eventually, they'll find a new thing to occupy their time. I do mention Miranda, though, because I just can't not.

Me: *How did things end up with the real estate agent last night?*

Oliver: *I didn't meet with her last night, but we had a couple of video chats with some prospective sellers today.*

Me: *And? Is your dream closer to becoming a reality?* Please say no. Please say no.

Oliver: *Hard to say. I felt like I was being interviewed to be the people's nanny, personal shopper, and fiancé all rolled into one. They're not interested in handing their homes over to just anyone, that's for sure.*

What do I say? "I see?" "So, you're really going for it?" "You weren't being honest with me when you said it wasn't your dream anymore?"

But I can't do that. I can't ask him to give this up. He would need to come to that conclusion himself.

Me: *Sounds so cool, though! I hope it all works out for you!*

There. Isn't that what friends do? They support each other, even when the other person's dream kills their own.

I wait so long to get a text back from him that I almost fall asleep on Wilford's back.

Finally this: Oliver: *Thanks. We'll see. But like I said last night, I don't really want to buy a house in Capri anymore, except maybe as an investment.*

I don't know what to say.

Me: *Well, either way, I hope you get what truly makes you happy.* I swallow hard. A swirl of confusion is coating my tongue.

Oliver: *Thanks, Soph. I hope that for you, as well.*

I think we're both holding back. What I really want to text him is: Oliver, I love you. But instead, I write: *Wilford is doing a potty dance. If I don't take him out, I'll have a puddle on my floor. Goodnight, Oliver.*

I don't even check to see if he writes back. I can't.

Chapter 25

Oliver

I'm a grade-A coward. At least that's what Alec is telling me through the phone.

I've just stepped off the plane at Heathrow, and I'm exhausted, starving, and all things not pleasant. I can't shake the crankiness that has threatened me ever since Miranda showed up at the resort two nights ago.

I'm on the cusp of some huge changes in my life, and my old ways and my newfound purposes are at odds.

What did I do to work through that? I took a quick jaunt to London to clear my head. Our London location is a posh, smaller resort on the outskirts of the city, with that old-world, British vibe and a great view of the skyline.

Sebastian said to go, so I did. No big whoop.

Except, I didn't even tell Sophie anything about it.

If that's not enough to make me sick, my conversation with Alec does. He heard from Sebastian that I got roped into attending this shareholder meeting in London, so he figured he'd call me when I landed so we could go over all the latest issues behind the scenes of his former NFL team. It was a conversation that quickly turned to the subject of Sophie.

I manage to successfully steer the conversation back to Alec's life—twice—but as I'm being driven to our Tate International London location, he brings up Sophie again.

"Gonna harp on me about this?"

"Harp? There's no harping. Just showing interest in your life, is all."

"Wish you were more like Henry."

"Absent? Gee thanks, Oliver."

"No. But Henry minds his own business and it's a beautiful thing." It's not great that he's usually far removed from the family, or that we often don't know where he is or even where he's living, due to his top-secret job.

But in moments like this, I sure wish Alec would back off a little.

"Tell me why you thought it was okay to leave without telling her." At my groan, Alec continues. "I think if you unpack things a little, you might understand yourself better."

"If we could end this conversation, I could call her and tell her where I am, and everything will be fine."

I don't mention that I don't exactly believe that to be true. I also don't mention that when she told me to go for my dreams and live in Capri, it sure felt like that meant we weren't a thing, or at least wouldn't be for long. My gut burns.

Which reminds me again of my cowardice.

"Mom's excited you two are dating. She said if you don't marry her, you're a total idiot."

"Marry her?" The truth is, that thought isn't as strange to me anymore. I always knew I didn't want to stop seeing Sophie every year. How that was going to work out when we both had a special someone in our lives wasn't something I was willing to think about. Now, I'd like my special someone and Sophie to be one and the same.

Alec chuckles. "You've known her long enough. I say just go for it."

"Sure wish you all would mind your own business."

"I just don't want this carefree attitude to come back to haunt you. Call her and tell her you weren't thinking straight when you chose flight over fight. Fix this."

"Alec, you're not allowed to give me dating advice."

"Except it's not just dating. This is *Sophie*."

"I know." The rock in my stomach at being so rash to hop on a plane to London without telling her is not sitting right.

"I don't think you get it, Oliver. She's not just some woman you're getting to know. Even I understand the need to let a woman you're in love with know when you're leaving the country."

I want to protest. I want to tell him I'm not in love with her. But I can't say that. I can't say much of anything because I know he's right.

I slouch down in the car that's stuck in traffic leaving London, wishing I was in Sophie's Corolla instead. I find myself daydreaming about that place where her hairline touches her neck, the hollow that curves away from her ear. The softness of her skin.

I should have told her I was going, like a real boyfriend would have. I could have even brought her with me.

When Sebastian told me to go to London for him—he didn't ask me, he told me—I pushed against it like someone who's offered a piece of cake at a formal event. You might outwardly balk at the idea because you're in a nice suit and representing the company and all, but you're secretly glad you get to eat a piece of cake!

So, yeah. I ran like the coward I am. I used to think it was so great that I never stayed in one place. All of us boys have responded to Tate International's success in different ways, but mine is to see the world and move swiftly from one place to the next, never feeling satisfied because there was always more, more, more.

There's never been a relationship to figure out, because there was always another place calling my name. But Sophie deserves better.

Everything hit me at once, and the thought of flying to London to clear my head was so appealing I went for it, without thinking.

As the car arrives at the London Tate resort, my stomach holds sludge. I did Sophie wrong and need to rectify it.

Chapter 26

Sophie

Oliver's not in his office, but the door is open and I let myself in. He must not be too far away because no one would leave the door to an office this nice unlocked.

I set up shop. It's already past six and I barely had time to scarf down some of Claire's frozen ravioli before coming here. The wood and paint scent that usually hits me was tempered with something else when I walked through the main entrance just now, and I think I've figured it out. I think it's the scent of the little, last-minute things this resort needs all coming together. I swear, readiness hangs in the air.

Except around the resort library area. That place reeks of uncertainty.

My projects tonight include tracking the book packages, setting up appearances with local authors, and keeping my heart as open as I can.

I think I'm ready for that last one. Not because I necessarily know how Oliver will respond, but because if I don't, I'll always regret it.

When my stomach rumbles from the cavern the few bites of ravioli opened up without satisfying, I snap my fingers in the air a few times. Maybe I can conjure up Drake, his beard, and his food.

When that doesn't work, I laugh at myself, but I also take my phone out of my pocket to text Oliver. I've been here almost an hour and still no sign of him. Maybe he and Miranda are finalizing his Italian beach front property right now—the thought of which makes me nauseated.

After I text Oliver to tell him I've arrived, I get up to stretch and then wander over to the library corner. I've stopped calling it a nook because the builder told us the ductwork and electrical behind one of the walls prohibited us from anchoring shelving there. So now it just looks funny, and honestly, it's a little depressing.

Not the feeling I was intending to invoke. But I wander over there anyway because what else am I going to do? My petition for a real live, brick and mortar library for Marshall County is sitting in some inbox of some council member and there's nothing I can do about it. And there's not much I can do about this nook right now, which fills me with a sense of loss. I'd been so excited about this project. It was something new and fresh and different. Now it's borderline pathetic.

I see that another box of books has arrived from the retailer, and I resist the urge to rip it open and take a big whiff. These babies have to stay put until mama's got the shelves up and their new home ready.

I'm creeping myself out with the babies and mama talk because this is exactly how I was afraid my life turn would out: instead of becoming an old cat lady, I'll become that old lady who talks to her books.

At least the nook, er—corner—has the furniture now. It's not arranged exactly right, but since I'm no interior designer, I'm going to have to play around with it some more.

I'm trying to shove one of the sofas with my shoulder when Britta walks by.

"Hello, Sophie. The, um, space is coming along nicely."

See? Even she can't call it a nook.

"Thanks, I'm getting excited." I rub a hand over the leather chair. "Have you seen Oliver? I could use his muscles to move this thing."

"I'll call someone up to do that for you." She slides her glasses tighter over her ears. "And didn't he tell you? He's in London for a couple of days."

"Oh." My heart skitters. I can't think of a single other response. Why hadn't he said something? London for a couple of days for me would have been the trip of a lifetime and something I would have told everyone about, including the kid who bags my groceries.

But this is just another day in the office for Oliver, right? People in his line of work do this kind of thing all the time.

Britta leaves to call someone to help me.

But he didn't tell you...but he didn't tell you...but he didn't tell you reverberates against my skull. Alarm mixed with frustration rings even louder.

Maybe I've misread things between us.

I feel small. Unimportant.

I need to get some of my aggression out, which is the only explanation for my shoving the sofa even harder with my shoulder. I don't need anyone else's muscles. I have quite enough on my own to do this job. As I'm aimlessly shoving against it, my feet sliding across the wooden floor, I see a pair of sneakers with bright colors.

The shoes are attached to Alec.

"Britta said you needed some help." Even though he's smiling, I'm not fooled into thinking he's feeling super content with his life. I don't even really know what he does for the company. This is the first time I've seen him in the building. He's dressed in workout clothes.

I stand from my odd pushing stance. "When she said she'd send some muscle to help me, I didn't know it'd be you, Alec."

"I was already on my way downstairs when I ran into Britta. It's really not a problem," he says.

I nod and swing my gaze around, feeling wholly inadequate to be asking him where the sofa should go. They really should have had their designer's input on this.

"It's starting to come together. I like it." Alec's gaze roams the area.

"Well, there's a lot more to do. I wanted to play around with things." I rush over to some boxes that hadn't gotten unpacked yet. "And these are the dinner trays that we're repurposing as places to set books. It'll give it a more relaxed and welcoming feel."

He nods and we work for a few minutes, trying and failing to find the exact right place for the sofa.

"It's a gorgeous piece of furniture." I run my hand along the butter of the leather. It's so soft I could cry. Or maybe I could cry because Oliver went to London without telling me.

"I see what Oliver meant." Alec is folding his arms over his chest, surveying the area with a strong sense of distaste. "This nook isn't working. It's just not...appealing enough..."

I'm torn, because I know he's right, but part of me really wanted to prove that I could do it, that I could make it better than it was. I wanted to pull a bouquet of flowers out of a hat.

"You just wait," I insist. "It's going to be much better."

"Oh, I know." He flicks a glance at me, and there's something gentle there. Understanding? Compassion? "I know this is important to both you and Oliver," he continues. He sighs and shifts his weight, placing his hands on his hips.

"We'll make it work," I assert. I hope the Tates don't decide to nix the whole project.

"I don't doubt you'll do the best you can, but—" He looks out the window at the darkening sky. "It's too bad the patrons' only view while they're in this spot is of the parking lot."

"Yeah," I say. "We'll figure it out." But will we? I know it's just a little space—not a big deal. It doesn't really matter much. But it's become significant to me. I have to see this through.

He frowns. "That's not okay." He growls lightly. "No one's going to want to read back here."

I don't know what to say, so I busy myself with reading and re-reading the packing slip from one of the boxes of lamps. Fascinating stuff.

"We'll figure out how to make this better. I mean, even moving all of this to face the wall instead might be a better alternative than a view of the parking lot." His phone buzzes and he glances at it. "When Oliver gets back, I'll have Sebastian join in and we can sit down and figure this out."

"Speaking of Oliver, do you know when he's getting back?" I hate the neediness I feel.

"I would guess sometime tomorrow." He sighs again. "Sebastian sort of forced the trip on him. One of us had to be there for the meeting, and he couldn't go this close to our grand opening." He glances at his phone again and then shoves it in his pocket.

"I have to go. I'm supposed to discuss some produce issues with the chef. But can I just say something? I think you're a really great person and Oliver...well, there's sort of this thing—"

My heart hammers in my chest. "A thing." I repeat, my voice flat.

"It's a Tate thing." Alec hesitates. "From the past. Our father has always cautioned us against dating people from the company."

I laugh. "I'm not from the company. I'm freelancing for like a month and besides, I don't know how serious this is—"

He gives a grunt of a laugh. "Well, we'll see..."

"No. I mean, yes. We're good. He and I are good. Except I don't know if I can talk about this right now."

"Of course. Well, freelancer or not, maybe you should contact HR if you want to continue with the relationship."

It's odd that I'm having this conversation with Alec, and I want to ask him what he means by 'a thing from the past.' But before I can, he answers his ringing phone, nods in my direction, and covers the phone with his hand. "We'll meet up with Sebastian and Oliver soon," he says to me before he disappears into the elevator.

The doors barely close before I take my phone out of my pocket. I call Oliver, and as it rings over and over, I'm torn. I have the right to my anger over his dissing me, don't I? Or am I merely a small blip on the trajectory of his life, with no claim on him at all?

Chapter 27

Oliver

I'm in the meeting. I'm here. I made it. That doesn't mean I give a rat's behind about what's being discussed.

I've got Sophie on my mind.

I messed up.

I type out practice texts, careful not to send them yet, trying for a breezy tone like, "Hey, Soph, you'll never guess where I am!" A groan of frustration exits my lungs because I know that won't cut it.

The meeting goes on a ten-minute break, so I stand and tug my hand through my hair. It was a mistake to not tell her I was leaving, and my impatience with myself is growing. I pace back and forth along the business room's corridor, wondering how I can make this right.

What is wrong with me? Why did I run? She deserves so much more than me. She needs someone who isn't terrified at the thought of something deep and real.

That's always been the reason, hasn't it? My go-to thought has been, *I can't have a real relationship because I don't have the first clue how to have one.* My parents' marriage has scared me, there's no doubt about that. But what if that's been my crutch all along? Just because they're dysfunctional, doesn't necessarily mean I'll be, does it? I have the advantage of having seen it my whole life. I know what I want, and it's completely different from what they have. Knowing that is an advantage in my favor, right?

I don't know. But I do know I don't want to be without Sophie. I love her. And if she'll have me, I want to be with her for the rest of my life.

How are we supposed to figure this out, though? Because Longdale is problematic. I think Sophie was right when she said she's worried about how I'll feel about it in the future.

When shareholders begin filing into the room again, the guilt's boiling up to new heights. I have to contact her, but words seem so inadequate. The truth is, my actions have placed us in the category of boss and employee, or just casual friends.

That's wrong. And sending her a text during my meeting won't fix any of it.

I miss Sophie. I can't wait to go back.

I'm at her doorstep. The house screams Sophie. Small and cozy, the brick is painted white. The shutters are macaroni and cheese orange, and the wooden door is stained dark brown. There's a metal sign on the porch that's in the shape of a Bernese Mountain Dog that says, "Don't Stop Retrievin'."

I chuckle despite myself, and despite the harsh vibes I'm getting from Sophie's sister, Claire. "Do you know where she's headed today?" I ask.

Claire sighs and folds her arms. "No idea. One of the towns in the county. Does that narrow it down for you?"

Never buddy buddy with me, Claire's loathing is dripping off her like acid rain.

"Uh. Yes. At least now I know she's at work." I venture smiling at her, but it doesn't do anything to ease the discomfort between us.

"Why don't you just text her and ask her where she is?" She glances down at my disheveled appearance. I realize I look jet lagged, but I didn't have time to do anything about it. I came here straight from the airport, only stopping in the bathroom to change out of the pants I was wearing since there was an incident with a kid's juice box on the plane.

Yes, I flew coach next to a toddler in his dad's lap because I exchanged my first-class ticket on a later flight for an earlier one and beggars can't be choosers.

I have to see Sophie ASAP and apologize for running. When I'm stressed about something, I run. I always have.

"I'll text her," I say to Claire. "Or I'll look up the schedule on the website. Thanks."

I'm not even back to the car before I've got the schedule pulled up. Fairhill. She's in Fairhill today.

It's when I'm safely on Lakeside Road, forest on either side of me, that I punch in a call to Sophie.

No answer. I mean, she is working. That's probably why she's not answering. But it puts a staccato note on my fear. I ache for her to understand. I ache for her, period.

Twenty minutes later, I see the mobile library on the side of the road, tilted at an angle. Oh no. I'm going too fast to stop in time, but I slow to do a U-turn. At first, the angle of the big, brightly colored bus makes me think it has a flat tire, but as I pass it, my eyes scanning for Sophie, I see the hood is popped open.

It takes me several seconds to slow down enough to turn around, and by the time I'm heading back towards Scott, my mind is racing. Where is Sophie? What's wrong with the bus?

I park my car near Scott's hood, so I can jumpstart the battery if needed.

"Sophie?" I call out as I walk around the perimeter. "Soph, are you okay?"

I clamor up the metal ramp and in through the open door.

"Oliver? What are you doing here?"

She has her hands on her hips. She's wearing white and blue striped men's pajamas and they're cut in such a way that they cling to her body in all the right places. I nearly stumble as I walk towards her—she's so beautiful.

I want to catch her up in my arms, but I stop myself. "I just got back from a last-minute trip to London. Are you alright?"

She nods. "When I got my CDL," she says, "They didn't include any info about how to repair this dang thing."

I smile. "Did it overheat?"

"I don't think that's the issue." But then she steps back and away from me, changing the subject. "You look...not so great. Britta told me about your trip."

"I'm so sorry I didn't say anything. I wanted to call or text while I was there, but nothing seemed adequate. There's so much I need to say, Sophie."

She frowns. "I tried calling you, but you didn't answer."

"What? When?" I take my phone out of my pocket and scroll through my call history.

"Yesterday." Clearing her throat, she waves me away. "It doesn't matter." She smooths the front of her pajama top. "I'm doing a story time pajama party today in Fairhill." She perks half a smile like she's embarrassed and then chews her bottom lip.

"I need to start coming to story time." I want her to know how beautiful she is. I've missed so many opportunities to tell her that.

She wrinkles her nose. "Except that might be bizarre."

I laugh. "Yeah, it might be." I look back at my call history. "I'm not seeing any calls from you yesterday or today. I wonder if it's because I was in London, and it didn't go through?"

My mind's shifting through so many thoughts and wishes that I can barely keep up. But I know she's trying to get to Fairhill. "What's wrong with Scott?" I glance around at the neat rows of books, cozy overstuffed chair, and funny book posters. "The inside looks great." I want to touch her hair, her hand, her lips...any part of her would do.

"It was built when we were still in junior high, that's what's wrong with it." The way she purses her lips together has me cracking a smile.

"Well, let me see." I head out and down the ramp. "If you'll turn the engine on," I shout. "I'll take a look."

"Are you an expert on engines?" She joins me outside, her brows raised. She challenges me with a look. There's something brewing in her countenance.

"My grandpa taught me a few things," I say. I peer into the engine compartment before glancing at her.

A look I can't decipher crosses Sophie's face.

"What?" I ask her. "Why is that so hard to believe?" Before she answers, I start to roll up my already wrinkled sleeves.

"It's not that hard to believe."

"So, then why the look?"

A soft sigh trickles out her own vulnerability. "Oliver. You're not supposed to be able to fix buses."

"I didn't say anything about fixing Scott, Soph. All the Sunday nights of my life in my grandpa's garage wouldn't prepare me for that."

"Ouch." She frowns and pats the hood. "What are you saying about my sweet ride here?"

"It's not a commentary on your ride—I'm talking about my poor skills. And what did you mean when you said I shouldn't be able to fix cars?"

She joins me at the engine, and her hip in those attractive pajama bottoms leaning up against the grate. "It's just that it surprises me when I find out something new about you."

"Why is that a bad thing?" I can't look her in the eye. I really want to, but I almost don't want to know what's behind her words.

"It's not bad. Just complicated."

I wish I could pull her close, but already my fingertips have dirt on them from brushing my hand along the battery. Besides, I need to talk with her somewhere besides the side of the road next to her busted up bus.

"I've told you I thrive on complication," I say.

"Which is probably why Sebastian asked you to go to the U.K." There's a heaviness between us.

"Exactly. But if you'd rather me not look at the engine—just look, of course— then I'll close the hood and call a mechanic."

"No. It's okay. I mean..." Her voice breaks a little. "It wouldn't hurt to take a peek." She seems genuinely worried about Scott.

And we've been talking in circles so much I don't know if we've been referring to the trip or the bus or none of the above. And I can't go on before I give her an abbreviated version of the thoughts swimming in my head. "Before I do, about London—" I stop short. Where do I even start? "I sincerely apologize for not letting you know in advance. Sebastian only gave me a few hours' notice before takeoff, but that's no excuse. I should have told you where I was going. I should have said goodbye and helped you with anything you needed beforehand—" Regret simmers in my chest.

"It's okay." She glances at the hood of the bus, and her face is vacant.

I know when to move on. Temporarily. There's a storm underlining her words and no matter how much I try to focus on other things, I'm not going to be able to run from it forever.

I study the engine, but honestly, I can't tell if things look right or wrong. "Can you start it up and we'll go from there?" I ask.

"That's the problem. The engine sounds like a dementor procreated with Metallica."

I laugh, but she cringes before turning towards the ramp.

It only takes a few seconds after the key is turned in the ignition for my stomach to wrench. "Okay, you can turn it off," I yell through the banging noise.

The mobile library is toast.

When I tell her I'm pretty sure it's thrown a rod, her face grows white.

"I had a car in high school that threw a rod and I'll never forget that ungodly sound." I shudder at the memory. "I'm really sorry." I tell her I can give her a ride to wherever she needs to go. She gives a hollow laugh and starts typing mercilessly on her phone.

"I can't have a pajama day story time without the bus."

I start to ask her how she can have story time in the cramped bus in the first place, but stop myself. Now is not the time for details. She interrupts my thoughts, and as per the usual, she knows what I was thinking. "We have it outside. I roll out the canopy and throw down some carpet squares. The kids love it."

"Want to have it at the resort? I'm sure we can find a space for it." I absolutely don't want to do it in the library nook, though. There's no room for carpet squares.

"Thanks, but it's happening in less than an hour. And no one's going to want to drive there from Fairhill." She takes a deep breath and looks down at the keys in her hand. "I hate canceling, but..."

"It is a shame, especially because no one gets to see these nice pajamas."

She shakes her head. Nope. She's not feeling my compliments right now.

"Can you drive me back to the county offices so I can get my car?" she asks, smoothing her hands down her thighs.

"Now, wait just a minute. Story time in Fairhill has to happen, Soph."

She throws a hand in the air in the direction of Scott. "You said yourself the bus is in bad shape." I think eventually she'll cry about this. But right now, she's in the anger stage.

"No," I say. "Not today, dementors and Metallica. Not today."

I'm in full-on rescuer mode and it feels so good. Sophie watches as I make the phone calls, her hands wrapped around her middle and her face scrunched up. Within minutes, I've got a tow truck on its way. We grab the carpet squares and a few picture books about bedtime and teeth brushing and put them in the trunk of my car. The tow truck arrives, hooks up Scott, and we peel out before them. I'm not going to drive on the mountainous part of Lakeside Road behind their cautious snail's pace.

On the drive, I manage to get her laughing about a song on the radio and about a memory of the time we dared each other to skip to Stella's from the shake shop after we got off an early shift. Skipping all that way was no joke. We were sore for a week.

We're only a couple of minutes late to story time, but we set up quickly. A few minutes after Sophie starts to read, the tow truck pulls the bus up, very slowly, and settles it a safe distance behind her. The kids are fascinated by the whole process.

When Sophie starts in on the next book, I see there's one extra carpet square that I can claim—at a sufficiently uncreepy distance from the toddlers and their moms. I feel out of place because I'm in my disheveled clothes and not my pjs like everyone else. But thankfully, I'm not sitting so far that I can't enjoy the straight masterpiece that is Sophie in her element.

She's funny, with different voices for each character and the perfect number of dramatic pauses. My favorite thing is watching her eyes as she laughs with the kids—bright and joyful.

My second favorite thing? The way the moms and kids all come up to her when it's over, giving her high fives and thanking her like she's a celebrity. My chest burns at this.

Thanks for recognizing her brilliance, Fairhill.

After everyone leaves, we make arrangements with the tow truck driver and soon, he's ready to tow Scott back to the county offices. On our drive back to Longdale in my car, she's quiet for a few minutes before speaking up. "Thank you, Oliver." She swallows hard and blinks rapidly.

"I'm glad it worked out. Listen, Soph. I'm sorry I didn't let you know about the trip. I just want to say that, Sophie, I care about you. A lot. And not even telling you I was leaving was the wrong way to show you that."

Her smile is humorless. "You're not obligated to tell me anything."

"Yes, I am." I swallow, and my throat is thick like I've been stung there by a bee.

"It did bother me." She gazes at the trees as we pass them. "But you're here now, aren't you?" She reaches for my hand, the one that's not on the steering wheel, and gives it a squeeze. Before I can say more, she speaks. "I've got to let the county know about Scott so they can call a mechanic."

The euphoria I felt leading up to and during story time is diminishing. And I feel sick worrying about the direction things might take, and if I'm going to be able to fix it.

Chapter 28

Sophie

I'm at home, on my sofa, holding up the phone close to my face. Joe Driggs and Dora Slater are droning on about something on speaker, but it's hard to focus on their words.

"I'm sure this isn't what you wanted to hear. I'm sorry, Sophie." Joe does sound genuine.

As is the case with many of the council members, I've known these two for as long as I can remember. When my mom got sick, Joe came and mowed the lawn and brought us meals on occasion. Dora taught band at the high school, and even though I totally sucked at the clarinet, she was always kind and encouraging to me.

"Look on the bright side," Dora cuts in and I can tell she's grabbed the phone from Joe. "Eventually, once everything gets sorted out, you'll get a brand-new vehicle to drive around. Eventually."

I know I complained about Scott being a blight in my life. But what am I supposed to do now? *Come back to me, Scott! Come back to me.* Besides, what about the petition for a brick-and-mortar location? Have they all forgotten about the list of signatures I gathered?

"How soon do you think the county can get another one?" I ask.

There's a long pause on the other end, and then I hear the phone being manhandled and covered up, with muffled whispers shooting back and forth. I'm half tempted to hang up. Because of the amount of time it's taken them to argue over my question, it's clear I won't want to hear what they have to say anyway.

When the bus broke down a few days ago, right from the get-go, it felt worse than normal. I've dealt with breakdowns through the years. But this time, with the unholy knocking sound, I knew. I just knew Scott was a goner.

I was in shock about it and then Oliver showed up, a knight come to save me. I could tell he was sorry he left for London without telling me, and the way he took over and had Scott towed—twice—was unbelievable. I could definitely get used to Oliver joining me at work. He made everything better.

But I can't shake that these issues with him are the tip of the iceberg. His response to his emergency trip to London feels like something much larger: a reminder of all the odds stacked against us. My grandparents are one issue, sure. The need to contact HR is another, and although that will be relatively painless, it's hard to bring it up with Oliver. Because then this thing we have would have to be defined.

And then there's another whisper of a concern: what Alec said about the past. I can ask Oliver about this. And I will. There are a lot of Tate brothers, so it wouldn't even necessarily be anything to do with him.

I just need to get it over with and ask him. Knowledge is power, right? Ignorance is, most certainly, not bliss. It's a tortuous state, where my imagination runs wild.

My thoughts are interrupted by the static on the other line and Dora's voice coming in again, this time, too loudly—she's got the phone too close to her mouth. "The purchase of a new library bus can't even be discussed until the next meeting with the county." There's so much pity in her voice that my head starts to throb.

"And when is that?" I ask, jamming my eyes shut to brace for her answer.

"Normally, just next month. But with Longdale Days and the summer in full swing, we usually take June off. So it won't be until July. The end of July." She pauses. "Oh, but since we take June off, that means July's meeting ends up being hours long just to get caught up. There's actually a good chance there won't be time to bring it up until August's meeting. I'm so sorry, Sophie."

August? I can't believe it. What am I going to do until then? And that's just when the meeting to decide what to do will be. Who knows when Marshall County will take action on the decision? And will I even be getting a paycheck until then?

When I don't answer, Joe cuts in. "For right now, we need to remove all the books and everything from the premise. It's going to be sold for its parts."

I suck in a deep breath.

"Now, Joe," Dora chides. "You don't have to say it like that. You're so brutal."

"Brutal? She deserves to know the truth."

"It's fine," I say, but I don't think either of them hear me. Dora's too busy getting after Joe.

"Of course she deserves to know. I just think since she's been our county librarian for, what's it been, over ten years, she's going to be sad about her bus being sold like that. It's traumatic."

Joe's laugh is gruff. "Traumatic? I mean, I can think of a lot of other things that would be traumatic. Unfortunate? Yes. But if I were her, I'd be relieved to be rid of the sorry sack of--"

"Joe!" Dora cuts in. "We don't know the future of the library program. There are no guarantees. I just think you could work on your delivery. I know Nancy feels the same way."

When Dora mentions the future of the library program, I get sick to my stomach again. The budget meetings every year always make me nervous. I never know if the budget line items to run the library will be renewed. But I've never been seriously worried before. I am now.

"You talk to my wife about me?" Joe tosses back. "And then bring it up on the phone with Sophie?" There's a long, pregnant pause. Like they just remembered I'm on the line.

Then Joe starts in again. "How about your delivery on that, Dora? Should we talk about your spouse now? Huh?"

I start to laugh. It's all good-natured. And the back and forth between them is so perfectly Longdale that I start feeling nostalgic for my town. Which doesn't make any sense at all. How can I be nostalgic for a place I'm currently in?

Longdale isn't gone, but if my relationship with Oliver progresses, I might be. I might have to leave, and I can't do that. I'm almost the same age my mom was when she died, and that truth is a dumbbell across my chest She loved this little town and all its quirks. She *was* this town, the lake, the sky, the ibis. She was everything that's here.

And that's the hardest thing of all.

Chapter 29

Oliver

Scott looks no less pathetic parked at the Longdale city offices than it did the other day on the side of the road to Fairhill. It's a piece of junk. But thanks to Sophie's vision, it served the people of Marshall County for a long time.

The whole thing was extraordinary, how she transformed it from nothing to something remarkable. I don't think most people ever even realized how much a labor of love the library was for Sophie, and how she created it out of thin air with sheer grit.

People did notice her dedication and intelligence enough to keep asking her for help, though. They know she's amazing, which is why they tried to sweet talk her into a thankless task: chairing Longdale Days. I'm so glad she stood up for herself and said no.

So, now here we are, Sebastian, Alec and me, to help her unload all the books. I think if it had been anyone else, my brothers wouldn't have agreed to come. It's only a couple of weeks until we open and Sebastian's busy. He doesn't manage the other locations anymore, but he still has final say on a lot of things. He has a lot on his plate.

And Alec? Well, he's been helping where he can. Except, he's been preoccupied with feeling depressed about his knee. Which translates into a lot of moping around, eating terrible food like those frozen Cheeto tacos you reheat in the microwave, and obsessively watching and rewatching film from his playing days. It's sad. And also annoying. You pile on top of that his heartbreak from losing his girlfriend back in college, and the guy's just a walking chip-on-the-shoulder mess. Which means doing some service for the community will be good for him, right?

I park my Mercedes, and my brothers and I get out. It's after five, which means most of the cars in the city and county offices parking lot belong to people who are here to help Sophie.

But I'm not prepared for the chaos I'm seeing as we try to enter the bus. There's a line of twenty or more people, passing stacks of books in a chain. Like a conveyor belt, people are passing them along until they reach the person at the bottom of the ramp, who's, in turn, loading them onto a dolly, which, when full, someone else steers over to the building.

I get territorial where Sophie is concerned. I know this about myself. And when I see people showing up for her, it's like the flipside of that. I don't know what to call it, except maybe a huge sense of gratitude. And something like pride.

Sophie squeezes past someone. "Oliver? You made it." The smile she gives me is everything, even though it's laced with fatigue and stress.

I survey the orderly chaos. "We wouldn't have missed it. Put us to work."

It's then that she notices Sebastian and Alec. "Oh, and you came, too. Thank you." She smiles, palming her ponytail to one side and rubbing her neck.

Oh, the blessed sight that is Sophie's neck.

"We can use you in a little bit," she tells us. "We're almost done with the books, but then we'll need to untether the shelving from the walls." She tightens her high ponytail, and in her t-shirt and jeans, she looks pared down, vulnerable.

I've hardly seen her lately. Since the bus broke down, she's been busy trying to get answers from the county and calling around and visiting local businesses to drum up funds for repairs or a new bus. I know she's really hoping for a building to house the library in, but none of us are holding our breath for that. She's still found time to work on the library nook project, but it's taken a back burner.

I pull her aside and we walk around to the other side of the bus. It's quieter here, and we're alone.

"I can't talk long," she says, gesturing to the crowd of people on the other side who've come to help.

"I know. I just wanted to touch base really fast." This is where I saw her crawling on her hands and knees on the ground. This very spot is where things started to shift for me, when I began thinking of Sophie differently than I ever had before. When I realized how much I'd missed her, only seeing her once a year, and how much I was drawn to her.

But I don't bring that up now. There isn't time.

"How's the opening coming?" she asks, and then chews on her bottom lip.

I'm distracted by the nape of her neck. "Really good. Insane. Have you heard anything about another location for the library?"

At this, her face crumples, and she takes a steadying breath. "Just that they won't even be able to make a decision until July or August." She shrugs. "I don't know what to do. I mean, I always knew my Scotty boy would give up the ghost eventually. I just thought we'd already have a plan in place." She rests a hand on the bus's frame.

"Is there anything I can do?" The thought that she won't have work for a few months gives me both a shot of giddiness and a ton of reservations. I'm sad for her, but hopeful at what this could mean for us.

She shakes her head and licks her lips. "You're here, helping me unload everything. That's all for now. Except, I did have a question." She pauses. "The other day Alec was helping me with some of the furniture at the resort and he told me I should sign something with HR? I wasn't sure if...well, I thought I'd ask you about it."

"Huh." I wonder why he hadn't said anything to me. "I think we should sign whatever they need. Whatever says I can be with you." Even as the words tumble out, I wish I could take them back because her face is locked down, her lips pale. Her eyes squeeze in agony.

"Has—has this happened before?" The pitch of her voice rises. "He mentioned something in the past that made it necessary to do this, and I realized I know almost nothing about your past relationships, Oliver."

Instantly, I know what he's referring to and my heart goes cold. I shoot out a breath, my mind tumbling back in time. Why Alec went there confuses me. This was a family thing, no one else needed to be involved. And it was long dead and gone. "Look, Sophie. There was something that happened in the past in our family. Before we started Tate International.

It has nothing to do with me, though. I can promise you that. I want you to know I've never done this before—dated employees of the company, or co-workers." My gaze is steady. "Or freelance consultants."

She nods once, and glances over to the bus. There are three windows on this side that are still functioning as windows. The rest of them have been sealed over to accommodate the stacks. Sophie's sister, Claire, opens a window and leans her head out. "The Tate brothers—" she gives a nod to me. "—the other ones, are helping us finish faster. Where were they hours ago, right? Anyway, what would you like us to do next?"

"I'll be right there," Sophie says to Claire, her voice strained and unnatural. Claire moves to close the window, staring me down before she slides it shut.

I still haven't won her over, but I will. I have to. Anyone important to Sophie is important to me.

"I know we have to get going on the next project, but I wanted to say, there's a lot we should discuss," I ache to pull her into a hug, but I can tell she needs some space. "You can ask me any question about my past. My relationships, anything and everything, and I will answer them as completely and honestly as possible. But I do want to say it's too bad about the bus, that it couldn't be saved."

Tears glisten in her eyes. She swallows hard. "Yes, it is. And it kills me that the readers of Marshall County are going to be unable to check out books this summer. Logistically speaking, it's going to be the fall until we can secure a new place, mobile or not."

I only nod. Nothing I can think to say right now would be any help to her.

We begin to walk around to the other side of the bus. "The good news is, once this gets cleaned out, I'll be more available to you to help you with the opening. I'm all yours in a matter of days, Oliver." She brightens a little. "I'll even clean toilets if that's what you need me to do."

"I like the idea of you being all mine." I can't help it. I've fallen hard. And all of the uncertainties of the future be darned, because I can't not say it. "But I'm not letting you clean toilets."

She does a little cheer with her hands in fists. "I'm relieved to hear that. I was scared you'd take me up on that offer." She laughs and gives me a quick quirk of a smile.

I open my mouth to respond, but then we both stop short, surprised at who's standing in front of us.

I grunt and Sophie gives a little gasp.

"I didn't know you were in town," Sophie says.

Chapter 30

Sophie

I admit it. I tend to overreact. But I feel I've been very levelheaded where my grandparents are concerned. Yes, they intimidate me and push every last button I have, but they did raise me from the age of nine on up, and they did make many sacrifices to give Claire and me what we needed throughout our lives. If I hamster ball it up, I can usually make it through any encounter with some appreciation and dignity. Usually.

Which is why it's surprising that the first thing I want to do when I see them approach my mobile library is cry.

Batten the hatches! Steel yourself! Inflate that hamster ball right back up where it belongs!

I have to find my strength. They aren't supposed to know about whatever this is with Oliver. I have to think fast.

Then why are my feet cemented to the blacktop of the county offices? Why is my mouth too slackened to form words right now?

"Well, hello, Patricia. Vernon." Oliver's voice is bright. He's ever the cheerful businessman. They're just staring at him, as slack jawed as I am. "It's been a while."

He laughs, and I have to glance over to see if he's lost his ever-loving mind. Nope. He seems lucid enough, calm even. But I know his tell—the vein in his forehead—and it's beginning to appear.

They don't move to respond, so he keeps going. "It's good to see you." He reaches out a hand.

How? How can he be so easy breezy? And in a sincere, non-threatened way? These people loathe everything about him, and he's not worried about that?

My grandma's face goes white, and my grandpa's face goes reddish purple, and if circumstances were any different, I might have found that funny. Right now? My throat's got a firebrand pressed to it.

Oliver drops his unshaken hand. It's my grandpa who finds his voice first.

"And you're here because...?" He tilts his head toward Oliver, leading with his ear.

The heat from Oliver's arm next to mine emboldens me. "He's here for the same reason everyone else is, to help unload all the books."

My grandma clucks her tongue. "We heard about the bus breaking down. We're sorry, dear."

I nod. "Me, too. It's been a really good ten years. I'm sad to see it go."

"Mr. Tate," Grandma hones in on him. "I'm actually glad we ran into you here. It will save us some work..."

She pauses as my grandpa grumbles something under his breath. After a quick glance in his direction, she goes on. "We're asking you to cease and desist any interactions with our granddaughter for the foreseeable future."

What? My mind is tripping over "cease and desist." Is this a joke?

"And why is that?" Oliver has crossed his arms over his chest. It's a good look for him, as it accentuates his biceps and forearm muscles. His face is still calm and breezy. No wonder he can negotiate land deals so handily. Nothing seems to faze this man.

Just then, Oliver's brothers come out of the bus, carrying either end of one of my bookshelves. It's the most dinged up one, the one that held my classics, some fairy tale collections, and our tiny reference section. I don't even know where those books are now...in some pile in some random room in the county building, no doubt. My stomach travels up and up, until my head is swimming with a shot of grief.

I love my books—er, the county library's books. But those old bookshelves? Why am I sad to lose them? Oliver must sense my distress because he gently places an arm around me.

My grandparents seem thrown off by the appearance of not one, but two more Tate brothers. Before Grandma can answer, Grandpa chimes in. "Yes. A cease and desist. We wanted to give you a chance to hear us out before we sent an official letter. Maybe we can avoid the unpleasantness of that and just have a verbal agreement."

Oliver moves to respond, but I stop him. "No, that's not okay," I say to my grandparents. I laugh at the absurdity of this. "That doesn't make any sense. I'm not your dependent anymore. I haven't been for fifteen years. Even still, you could have voiced your concerns to me privately."

I can feel Oliver's gaze on me and everything in him tenses. I know he's holding back. As they pass, Alec and Sebastian stare pointedly at Oliver, an unspoken code being sent and received.

"We've never approved of your association with the Tates, but then when we lost the bid to build the turbines—" Grandma shoots out a breath. "Sophie, you know our business hasn't yet recovered. I don't understand how you can do this to us. You're helping them with the very thing that has harmed our family?"

"You know we own the house, Sophie." Grandpa's voice is menacing. He looks from side to side at the various Longdalers milling about. They're bringing objects out of the bus, certainly, but their real goal is to hear what's going on.

I can't go there in my mind. That my grandpa could possibly threaten me by bringing up the house is...well, I didn't think he was capable of that.

By now, Oliver's brothers have returned from the county offices, and they flank Oliver and I on either side. My grandparents' gazes bounce back and forth among all four of us.

I see something in my grandparents' faces that I don't know if I've ever seen before, or taken the time to notice. There's an element of fear there. It's as plain as day to me now. The Tates are the most insidious of enemies in their minds, so of course they don't want me to be around them.

We're interrupted by some of the community members, asking what more needs to be done. "I think there's a couple of people left in there," they tell me. "Violet's been giving us jobs."

"Oh." I think hard. "If everything's out of there, you can go home." I lean over to give them hugs. "Thank you so much."

"We got you," Tahlia Frandsen says. She owns the corner deli. I've probably spent half my paychecks in that place over the years.

Oliver is also thanking them, with big pats on the backs and laughter.

Once they get in their cars to drive away, I feel more level-headed, less venomous.

I turn back to my grandparents, willing myself to stay calm, objective. "What do you hope to gain from asking me to avoid all contact with the Tates?" My voice is softer now. I want to understand. And I don't want to bring up the house because maybe there's nothing to my grandpa's out-of-place comment.

"It's the principle of it," Grandma says with a hiss. "After all we've done for you."

The familiar pang of guilt resurfaces. But it wasn't my fault my mom died, and nothing they've done for me means I'm obligated to live my life for them.

"I'm very grateful for all you've done," I say, willing my voice to stay clear and strong. "And I can live my life as I choose."

Don't they understand that both of those things can be true at the same time?

"Liquidating the home might be the best option for us at this point, financially speaking, Sophie," Grandpa says. The lines on his face pucker together at his scowl.

"Sell the house?" My mouth is dry. Oliver tenses next to me, leaning forward like he feels ready to burst.

"We might not." Grandma lifts a shoulder and straightens her glasses. "Especially if we felt you were honoring your mother's memory by honoring our one request."

Their request? They'll sell the house if I don't stop associating with the Tates? They've gone and lost their minds.

Claire comes down the ramp, carrying bags full of papers from one of my drawers—papers I always thought I'd have plenty of time to sort through.

"Claire!" Grandma says. "I didn't know you were here, too."

Claire's mouth opens and closes twice as she hefts the bags down on to the blacktop. She glances at me before responding. "Sophie needs my help, of course I'm here. And I didn't know you were coming to Longdale. Is everything okay?" The hug that Claire gives them is stiff, her eyes questioning.

"Of course," Grandma says. "We're just here on a little business." Both she and my grandfather offer polite smiles.

"Good. We'd love any help you can give to the cause." Claire's cheeks dimple as she points to Scott. She always did know how to handle them better than I did. It's like I can't see past the big scars between us to see any good. Claire just has the natural touch.

Except, they look like she just asked them to taste test antacid brands. "Well, I suppose we could for a moment, but we can't stay long," Grandpa says.

My skin is itching all over from the family drama. The Tate brothers look supremely uncomfortable, too, but they're not going anywhere. "Great. Thank you," I say, starting to back away. I need a break. "If you want to just keep us company while we finish moving the last of it, that would be more than enough help." They're in their seventies. I'm not about to ask them to carry out the garbage bags or shelves.

I offer a stiff smile and spin on my heel. I run up the ramp to enter the bus, anxious to get a breather from my grandparents.

I'm not prepared for the gutted-out bus, wreckage from the last decade of my life, torn apart before my eyes. Some of the community members have even started ripping out the carpet, leaving the rusted subfloor exposed, broken.

I suck in my breath. Violet and her mother are removing my posters from the walls.

It's gone. Everything's gone. The past ten years of my life have been hauled out and stripped away.

Violet sees my stricken face. "Oh, Sophie. This must be so—"

"It's okay, I just—" I put up a hand, but can no longer speak.

She responds with something, but I don't hear her. I'm out of the bus, down the ramp, pushing past Oliver, his brothers, and my grandparents. I hear him call out to me, but I can't turn around. I reach my car and all I see is a blur. Roughly, I wipe the tears out of my eyes.

All I want is to be alone.

Chapter 31

Oliver

My mind buzzes as my brothers and I drive away from the county offices. I'm reminded again just how unhealthy Vernon and Patricia Hanson are, and a lump forms in my throat when I think of how hard things must have been for Sophie all these years since losing her mom.

However, I feel good about my conversation with them just now. We spoke after Sophie left, and it was brief and to the point. Now they know that my intentions with her are honest and true. If they choose not to accept it, she and I will have some decisions to make.

I know what I want, and I hope Sophie wants the same thing. Until I know for sure what she wants, I think I just need to act as if we're meant to be and go from there. I can't control her feelings, but I can make mine known. I can fight for her with every ounce of strength in me.

Because I love Sophie Lawson.

I arrive at her house. It's dark and her car isn't there. I call her, but she doesn't answer. If she wants space, I'll give it to her. But I have to know that she's okay. I'm guessing it was overwhelming to not only have the confrontation with her grandparents, but to see the state that Scott is in. Even I felt a little gutted at seeing it so torn apart, and I've hardly spent any time in there.

I try calling her again and this time she answers.

"Sophie? Are you alright?"

"Yeah." Her tone is harsh, and she doesn't sound okay.

"Are you home?" I look up and down the street to see if she parked there.

"No, Wilford and I are just driving around." She's quiet, but I can hear the rumble of her Corolla and Wilford's breathing.

After a long silence, I speak. "I know you must be in pain right now. I'm here for you, Sophie." I want to tell her I love her. It's right there, on my tongue, waiting to be shared. But I can't do that over the phone.

"I need to be alone right now, Oliver."

"I understand." There's so much I wish I could tell her, but I have to respect her need for solitude. "You know where to find me."

Back at the resort, things are utter chaos. There's a certain amount of adrenaline from being so close to opening. There's still so much to do. That Sebastian would even consider coming to help Sophie was surprising. Usually at this point in the process, he's in an all-out frenzy. Like, teeth bared and neck vessels pulsing.

After some time in my office, I go to find him and Alec, but I'm intercepted every time. It's past seven at night, and still, we have sous chefs coming in to place orders, painters to direct, housekeeper interviews to supervise.

It's not until late in the evening that things have calmed down enough that my brothers and I find ourselves in the lounge on the second floor. It has a balcony that overlooks the lobby, but despite the open feel, there's something about the way the room is situated that feels comfortable and secluded.

"You look terrible," Alec drawls. He's got a drink in his hand and he's massaging his bad knee with the other. Carrying out those bookshelves for Sophie was probably not the best idea because the guy refuses to ice or wrap his knee anymore.

I motion to his bum leg. "So do you, old man." Alec's the second youngest brother, but with him hobbling around, you can bet we all tease him about it.

The truth is, though, I'm sure Alec is right. I know I feel terrible. All the busyness of the day is done and now I just miss Sophie. A mood is threatening to descend on me, which is odd. I so rarely feel this way, I don't know what to do with it. I should ask Sebastian for pointers since he's the expert on bad moods.

"Where are we at with the employee count?" Sebastian asks me.

I answer him with the latest numbers I've seen, but then I shake my head. "But I'm done talking about work for the night. I say we make a new rule that business talk ends by ten."

"I'd have nothing left to talk about then," Sebastian deadpans.

"Exactly," Alec and I say at the same time. Alec grins, Sebastian glowers, and I stay neutral, still fighting the urge to go under with my melancholy.

"How's Sophie?" Alec asks.

"After ten, no more talking about women, either," I say.

"What else is there?" Alec says. He's uncommonly chatty this evening. Maybe being in Longdale has been good for him. I kind of think it has been for me. A little.

Regardless, I pin him with a look and he rears back. "Okay, okay. I saw her leave in a rush and I was hoping she was alright," Alec says. "That's all."

"Did you call her?" Sebastian asks. It's surprising that he's concerning himself with this.

I nod. "She needs some time alone."

"You can't screw this up, Oliver." Alec is giving me a hard look, his voice a warning.

I surprise myself by not lashing out.

"I know," I say and I hold out my hand to take a few swallows from his drink. He sighs but hands the glass over. "I want to make some big changes, guys." I take a sip. "She's worth turning over a new leaf for."

Alec frowns. "Turn a new leaf over for yourself, bro. But if it benefits her, then that's even better. You gotta do what it takes to keep her."

"I know," I say again. "Whatever it takes." I think that's my new motto, but I'm not going to tell them that. I move to say more, but we're interrupted by a loud pounding at the front entrance.

With thoughts of Sophie at the forefront of my mind, I bound down the curving staircase and into the lobby, trying to see in the dark if it's her. *Please let it be her.*

It's not.

"Milo?"

My youngest brother, still in college at Columbia, is standing at the door. He waves off what looks to be an Uber and grabs a suitcase. His hair is longer than the last time I saw him, a thick, glossy mane of medium brown that almost reaches his shoulders. He's got on a plaid shirt, cut off sweats, striped tube socks, and flip flops.

My stomach drops. We had no idea he'd be coming. "What happened?" I ask, thinking of my parents, of Stella, of our cousins.

"What?" Milo asks, hauling the suitcase up and stepping into the lobby.

"What's wrong? Why are you here?"

"Well, hello to you, too." He gives me a hug with lots of back slapping and then stows his bag in the corner.

"Sorry, but—" I rush to keep up with him as he's walking fast across the tile.

His gaze takes in the warm and sophisticated expanse of the lobby. He whistles. "This looks even better than the pictures."

One of my favorite things is getting to see the looks on people's faces when they walk in. It fills me with a level of healthy pride that few things can compete with.

"I finished my semester and didn't want to go to Denver. No one's home right now."

"Where's Gabriel?" I ask.

My dad doesn't have a favorite son. This is something we can all agree on. Having a favorite would mean he's taken the time to get to know us, and that certainly hasn't happened. But if he were to have a favorite, it would be Gabriel—hands down. Where Sebastian is arguably the most successful, Gabriel's the one son who didn't leave home for good after high school. He helps Mom and Dad manage their charity work. He also sucks up to Dad. We all joke that he's probably the one son who hasn't had to deal with Dad blowing a gasket on the golf course mid-game.

"I think Gabriel's in Boston," Milo says. "Something about a children's hospital thing? Anyway, I figured I'd hang out with you guys."

We reach the loft sitting room, and Sebastian and Alec are just as surprised to see Milo as I am.

"What's wrong?" Sebastian asks, a growl coming from his chest. Looks like he's assuming the worst, like I was.

"Nothing's wrong." Milo grins. "I know it was forever ago that you all were in college, but don't you remember finishing the semester and feeling carefree?" His arms go wide. "I decided to spend some time with you."

I can't help but smile.

"I'm starving. Is the kitchen stocked yet?" Milo steps in to give Sebastian and Alec a hug. With Alec, they add on some sort of bro handshake.

It's nice to see that. Because he's the youngest, we all worried about him when Alec left home, being alone with our dysfunctional parents.

And it's clear Alec didn't know Milo was coming either. "Have a seat. We'll get you something to eat." Alec slings an arm around Milo as they walk over to one of the sofas, shooting Sebastian a look. He grumbles, but picks his phone up from the coffee table.

After a minute, Sebastian stares at Milo. "I asked Drake to find you something."

Milo grabs a throw pillow from the corner of the sofa he's on, punches it a couple of times and then tries to shape it into a ball. He lies down on his back, resting his head on it. He kicks his flip flops off and extends his legs across me so that his feet are resting on the arm rest.

He looks…downright sloppy happy.

One look at Alec's grin as he's staring at Milo and I burst into laughter. Alec joins in, and even the corners of Sebastian's mouth start to curve up.

"Where are Gabriel and Henry when you need 'em?" Milo says. "I don't want to play two-on-two. I wanna play three-on-three, like the old days."

Even though Milo's clearly in a good mood and the vibe in the room is a lot more upbeat since he arrived, his words send my heart plunging into my gut. I don't remember the last time we were all together, at least for longer than half a day at Christmas time. I even miss my parents.

I hadn't wanted to come to Longdale. I wouldn't have if Sebastian hadn't insisted. Something here was haunting me, something from my childhood. I don't want it to have ahold of me anymore.

Can I get rid of it if I don't know exactly what it was?

With a dash of grief, I realize that I probably can't.

"I've missed you guys," Milo says.

Sebastian nods his head. Alec and I say, "Me, too," at the same time.

We're quiet until Drake brings up a brown paper bag. We invite him to hang out with us, but he declines, straightening his man bun. "I've got a weight-lifting class at six tomorrow morning. I'm going to bed." Drake was given a room here in the resort so he can be on call for Sebastian much of the time. It's a pretty sweet gig, if you ask me. I wouldn't mind having my only two jobs be to supply Sebastian with food and run his errands.

Except then I'd have to be around Sebastian most of the time.

Milo digs in with gusto, chewing on marinated chicken thighs. I start thinking about what he said about missing us and wishing we could play three-on-three basketball like the old days, and suddenly, my mind is turning. A burst of energy pulses through me. I mean, I usually have a lot of energy. But right now? I could fly.

And just like that, I know what I'm going to do.

I'm ready to put things into place. My head's so dang clear, I feel like it's been squeegeed. Frankly, I'm a little frustrated with myself. Why hadn't I believed in this before? Why hadn't I decided this before?

I'm anxious to leave so I can start the process. First things first, I need to pay a visit to Stella. And then make some phone calls. Some very important phone calls.

But I don't leave quite yet. Four of the six of us are together now, and this is cause for celebration. I want to enjoy this. Alec starts to talk about the latest drama with the San Antonio Wolves, so I stay for a while longer before I start in on the rest of my life.

I want to listen. I want to help.

Chapter 32

Sophie

"There you are," Claire says to me as I walk in from the garage. Her gaze is glued to me, her mouth turned down in a frown. She calls Wilford over and rubs under his chin. "Go eat your food," she tells him, pointing to his filled bowl in the corner of the kitchen.

He's an obedient, good, big boy. Soon the only sound in the house is him noisily slopping through his food.

"The bus looked terrible," Claire says as I slump into a chair opposite her at the table.

"Like some flip job gone wrong," I agree. The sadness of it all comes crashing down on me again. "It's the end of an era and I'm not ready."

Claire nods. "When a door closes, a window opens up, though."

She's got some strong positivity vibes going, but I'm not ready to receive them. "Except where the Marshall County library is concerned, this closed door might mean the whole house is ready to be demo-ed and all the windows dashed to pieces."

"They haven't exactly made it easy on you to run the library program, have they?"

I shake my head. "And I'm not giving up the fight. It's just that I have no idea where to go from here. I'm tired."

"Does Oliver have any thoughts on the matter?"

"I wouldn't know." He called me after I'd come home, grabbed Wilford and his leash, and started driving around. "He's giving me space, like I asked him to."

"I saw his face when you were leaving tonight," Claire says. "Misery. Pure misery right there." Claire's talking about misery, but her face lights up. I never thought I'd see that from her where Oliver was concerned.

I lean back in my chair. "Did he say anything? Is he alright?"

Claire shrugs. "He didn't say anything to me." She rests her arms on the table, leaning towards me. "Sophie, why are you here in Longdale?"

If she's trying to change the subject so I won't be so distraught, it's not working.

"Born and raised, Claire. Just like you."

"Does it have to do with Mom?"

For a long time, it felt like everything had to do with Mom. Every decision, every feeling, had the essence of her woven into each thread.

I think for awhile. "You mean because she was an avid reader? That because she read to us, I became a librarian?"

Claire closes an eye and tilts her head. "That's maybe part of it. But why are you still here in Longdale, in this house, when the man you've loved half your life has been somewhere else?"

I start to protest, and she cuts me off with her hand in my face. "Indulge me. I just want to know why."

"He—" I swallow. "He's only recently started to feel that way." I peer at my fingernails. "Besides, this is my home. It's where I belong. Where Mom should still be."

"She's still here. And I'm not just talking about her gravesite. She's still watching over us, right? No matter where we go." She sighs and then worries her lip. "Sometimes, I wonder if Grandma and Grandpa did us a disservice by moving into this house instead of taking us back to their place in Boulder." She shakes her head. "I'm not ungrateful. That would have been incredibly difficult to lose mom and our house, neighbors, and friends all at once. And I know that's why they did it. They wanted us to have some stability."

Tears burn my eyes and throat. "I know. For all their...emotional distance...they did a lot for us."

"Yes. They're not warm like Mom, but they have their good qualities. Doesn't mean we have to put up with the unfair treatment, though." Her lips quirk up in a smile. "Boundaries, man. Am I right?"

My head aches. "They said something tonight, something about needing to sell the house," I say. "If I didn't stop working with the Tates." I massage my temples.

"They threatened to sell the house?" She squeezes her mouth shut and takes in a deep breath through her nose.

I nod. "That's not acceptable of them, Claire."

"I know." Claire stills, her expression boring into me. "But you can leave Longdale if you want, Sophie. I'll be just fine."

"Well, you can leave, too. Why are you still here and then getting after *me* for not moving on?"

"I want to move sometimes," she says. "I was staying to make sure *you* were okay."

We both laugh.

"You can run off with Oliver," Claire teases. "And I wouldn't even be mad if you eloped in some crazy place as long as you let me throw you a reception here eventually."

Her words shock me, but right now, I'm a puddle. My heart is beating wildly thinking about letting myself love him, completely, finally after all these years of telling myself I couldn't.

"Sophie, he's in love with you," Claire says.

"What makes you think that?" I feel a shiver throughout my bones. It's telling my body and soul that she's right. But that doesn't mean I can't ask her for her thoughts on the matter. I'd like to bathe in thoughts about Oliver and how he feels about me.

"After you left Scott tonight, he talked to Grandma and Grandpa."

I grip the edge of the table. "He did?"

Claire nods. "A nice, civil conversation. He was actually really good at validating their feelings, without letting them walk all over his own. He asked them to stop treating you that way. Sophie. He told them he was in love with you." Claire's eyes shine. "He promised that, if you felt the same way, he'd stay by your side. He said he wants to spend the rest of his life with you."

I cover my face with my hands. My heart is beating so wildly I can hardly think straight. "I can't believe it. Except. I *can* believe it, actually. That's the part that's so surprising...that I'm not surprised." I look at Claire. "He's never said he loves me. What did they say? How did they react?"

"Whoa. Hold up. You'll need to ask him about why he hasn't mentioned that yet. And as for Grandma and Grandpa? They said this will be difficult for them to accept, considering the past. But they said they were willing to try. Grandma was even smiling at the end."

This is all too much for me to take in.

"You should find Oliver," Claire says. "Go talk to him. He's worried about you."

"How do you feel about all this?"

She swivels her gaze up to the ceiling. "My only hesitation before was my fear that you'd get hurt. But seeing his face tonight—" She whistles and shakes her head. "He really does love you. And you can take care of your decisions yourself. I need to trust you in that."

"Thank you, Claire." I hug her, not able to stop the sting of tears in my eyes from all the pain and all the love that's been here in this house for so long.

Chapter 33

Sophie

I'm doing a strange, sort of wiggly dance as I get out of my car at Oliver's house. It's just nerves—the kind of nerves that buzz through my body like a cellphone on vibrate.

The early June sunshine has started to hit the treetops in Longdale. The air is so clean. My mind is so clear.

I sort of slept last night, even though every cell in my brain and body wanted to talk with Oliver.

I'm ready for this. I'm ready for all of it with him. And having to wait until this morning felt impossible.

I stand outside his house, reach my hand out to knock on the frosted glass of his modern-style front door, and then hesitate. For the first time in a long time, I don't have work today. I mean, with Scott being transported right this moment to a scrapyard upstate, I can't. It killed me to have to post on social media and the library website: "Library hours have been canceled indefinitely. Stay tuned for more information."

And that was it. Something about it feels so final, and I don't know if I'm just preparing myself for the possibility that the county will decide to forgo the library program altogether, or if I really do have a sixth sense about it.

In any case, nothing's holding me back now. Nothing's tying me down until at least August when the board meets. I'm free to love Oliver.

I knock on his door, not at all sure of what I'll say when he opens it. I glance down at the casual pants and tank top I threw on this morning, fingering the folded-up sheet of paper in my pocket. I did shower and wash my hair, so there's that. No juicy peach dog dry shampoo for this moment.

Before I'm quite prepared to see him, the door opens.

It's Oliver and he looks exhausted. And mildly panic stricken. His gaze goes to the luggage near the door, a suitcase, a carry on, and one of those squishy soft neck pillows. My tongue tastes sour. My mind goes a mile a minute.

He's leaving? I pushed him away yesterday, and now he's taking me at my word?

I've ruined everything.

I fight the urge to succumb to complete madness.

This is it, folks. The part where Sophie Lawson's every fear comes true, and she goes bat crap crazy.

But just like that, his smile appears, the one reserved just for me. He steps to me and wraps me in a tight hug. "Good morning," he says in my hair. Before I can answer, he moves back enough to see my face, like he's asking for permission.

The body is willing, but the mind still has about a hundred questions to ask.

"Where are you off to?" I ask him.

He glances at the luggage again. "I was planning this whole big thing as a way to tell you." He lets go of one arm that's holding me close and tugs at his hair. "But that's okay. I...we can do this right here, right now, if you want."

"I want...you," I say. Bravery from who knows where fills me up. "I want a life with you, Oliver. That's the only life I'm interested in. I don't care where we are or what we do, I just want you. That's all." I dig in my pocket for the paper and hand it to him.

He takes it and unfolds it, his eyes scanning the page. His mouth drops open, and then his goofy grin appears. "You applied for a passport?"

I nod. "It should be here in about eight weeks, and then I'm all yours. I'm willing to go wherever you need to go." I feel my eyes narrowing, and my heart starts to pound. "But it looks like you'll be leaving to go...somewhere...way before that."

He swallows and licks his lips. "I have to go to Capri. I've scheduled some meetings to wrap things up there. But I won't be gone more than three days, I can promise you that."

"Oh," I say. "Why? Why now?"

"Someone else can be boots on the ground there. It doesn't need to be me. There's a lot I have to finish before I can put someone else in charge of this project, though." He tugs me tighter to him. "But I want to take you there, when you get your passport. There's so much I want to show you."

I wrap him in an embrace, my hands sliding along his strong back muscles. Pure heaven. "I want to see it all."

The traffic light in my mind's eye is a bright, glowing, neon green now. I can do this. I can have hope in a future with the man I love. *Kiss me already, Oliver.* Everything else can wait.

Like always, he reads my mind. He moves in to kiss the bare edge of my shoulder. For a second or two, I can't think straight because all that's in my mind is one pressing thought: Oliver's kissing my skin.

Kiss.

Kiss.

Then, another kiss at the base of my throat. "So what do you think?" he asks quietly.

It's so unfair of him to ask me questions that require brain power when he's wielded me incapable of anything more than a moan.

Which escapes my mouth before I can stop it. In answer, he presses his mouth to mine. I feel him laugh a little against my lips. After exploring my lips with his, he breaks away. "I think I can safely take that moan of yours at face value."

I nod. "Yes, yes you can."

His smile is rakish as he moves back to me, nibbling at my jawline.

"I'm asking Sebastian about a more permanent position here at the Longdale Lake Resort."

A hundred tiny cheerleaders start doing back handsprings and waving pompoms in my head, but I rein it in. I do want to support him in his passions. Oddly enough, for the first time, I feel free...ready to leave Longdale for however long we need to.

"What changed your mind?" I ask. "Are you sure you can be here for awhile?"

We pull apart and he studies me carefully. "I talked to Stella last night. She thinks my hesitations with Longdale have something to do with some childhood trauma. This is where we came when things got really bad at home—every time." He shakes his head, chewing on his lip. "I don't know what to do with that, exactly, but at least I can see what she's saying. However..." His wolfish grin has me tingling. "Longdale's starting to grow on me."

I kiss him again. "How ironic. Just when you start to like it here, I feel the urge to leave." We laugh, and we're both wiping away the beginnings of tears in our eyes when he grows serious again.

"Soph, I talked to the real estate agent. I want to buy a house here in Longdale."

At my sharp intake of breath, he smiles.

"I was not expecting that," I say.

"I'm going to need your input. Basically, help me pick one out. Please?" He bites down hard on his back teeth, his gaze simmering with heat. "We could even purchase the house you're living in from your grandparents, if that's what you want." He kisses me, and there's a hitch to his breath. "I can stay at Alec's place for awhile until we...well, until we're ready to be together permanently."

"Mmmm. Together permanently? That's my favorite of everything you've said to me today." I just might want me to buy the only home I've ever known. Eventually. If we get married.

I'm so happy, so supremely happy.

He kisses me again, and I only pull away because I have one more thing to say.

"I love you, Oliver," I whisper. "I always have."

"I love you, Sophie." His eyes are gleaming with wonder. "And I always will."

Chapter 34

Oliver

Sophie is in my arms.

Midway through one of our epic kisses on the sofa of my rental, she gasps and pushes me away. "I almost forgot." She stands from the sofa. "Come with me," she says before making her way to the front door.

As long as it's with her, I'll go anywhere, but our long-time friendship necessitates some teasing. "The last time you told me to follow you, you gave me a spoon."

She throws her head back in a laugh. "Yes, I did. Prepare yourself because this might be even more exciting than that."

"I'm not sure that's possible."

At her protest, I press her closer to me. "I mean it. That you saved the spoon and had it in your car..." I shake my head. "It means a lot."

"Do you want to know what means a lot to me?" she asks. "Claire told me what you said to my grandparents. Oliver, to have you stand up for me like that is...it's overwhelming. It's incredible."

"I'll always stand up for you. I want to love you and protect you. Always."

Wherever she's taking me has to wait a minute or ten. Because now my lips are on hers again and I can't pull away.

She's made me promise to close my eyes, and I can feel her glance over at me every so often while she drives.

I feel the car slow and hear her flip on her blinker. As we turn, the surface of the road grows a little rougher, and I can smell the lake. It's something wild, carefree. It gives me images of childhood sandcastles and rafts, but the more recent memories with Sophie are at the forefront of my mind.

"Keep 'em closed!" she admonishes while climbing out of the driver's seat.

She opens my door and places her hand over my eyes. "Watch your head," she says after unbuckling my seatbelt. It's not until I've climbed out of the car and she removes her hand that I see where we are. "Shake, Shake, Shake?"

The purple plastic tables look to be scrubbed clean. The cement pad attached to the walk-up building has been power washed. A long line of customers snakes its way from the window.

"Hungry for a milkshake?" Sophie asks, threading her fingers through mine. Warmth radiates from her hand and up through my arm.

"It's the season's opening day?" I ask as we make our way to the end of the line. In the distance, Longdale Lake is crystal blue with foams of white along the rippling waves.

"Yes, it is," she says. She lets out a slow breath. "It's odd to think I don't have to drive Scott around. I feel kind of lost. And I'll have to go back to the county offices and organize everything...but not today."

"I've been thinking of a project you could do," I say. "Sort of a favor? In a way..."

Her expression is sassy. "Oh really? You need a favor, huh?"

I chuckle. "Yes. With so much time on your hands, I was thinking you could be in charge of a very important project at the resort. There's a room on the fourth floor that needs renovation..."

"Already? You haven't even opened yet, Oliver." But then it dawns on her, and her eyes grow large. "Wait—"

I nod, feeling giddy. "Will you turn my office into the resort library?"

"Really? Are you sure?" She does a little running dance move. "My secret pleasure has suddenly become resort libraries. You know this, right? Give me all the resort libraries!"

"Can't wait to see how it turns out." I join in her dance.

"But where will your office be?"

"I'll probably close off the existing library nook. Put in a door and call it good." I shrug. "I don't need anything fancy."

"No way. I'll convince Sebastian to let you have something else," she insists. She gives a squeal and claps her hands.

"My flight doesn't leave until tonight, so will you spend the rest of the day with me?" I don't like the thought of leaving her.

"Maybe I should stow myself in your suitcase and come along," she teases.

I answer her with a husky, "yes," and then wrap my arms around her. We meet together in a kiss, more perfect because we had to fight so hard for it.

After a moment, I slide an arm around her waist. "I know what we can do today," she says. "You realize since it's opening day of Shake, Shake, Shake, it's also the first day of Longdale Days."

"Oooo. Will you ride the Ferris wheel with me?" I ask. "We can eat an elephant ear, too."

"And I can beat you in the strongman game," she says. We laugh, but then Sophie tenses near me. I peer ahead and see her grandfather in line ahead of us.

"I got you," I whisper. She glances at me, offers a slight smile, and nods.

He purchases his over-the-rim milkshake and turns away from the shop. He takes a big bite of what looks to be strawberry cheesecake flavor when he stops short. "Sophie? Oliver."

She reaches out a hand to his shoulder. "Nice to see you here, Grandpa. Getting yourself a nice one on opening day?"

"Figured since we were in town, I'd make the best of it," he says in his blustery way.

We nod and step closer to the line. The air among us is awkward, but I can feel Sophie's strength next to me.

"Grandpa, I need to tell you that Oliver and I are together. He's a good man, and we love each other, and—"

He holds up a hand. "I know. He told me all about it last night." His mouth forms a harsh line.

She swallows hard. "I don't need your blessing, but I hope you can accept this. And accept that I can live my life the way I choose."

"I know," he says again. "Marie would have been proud of you."

His jaw is set, and his gaze steely. Despite his generous words, which I'm sure were difficult for him to say, I can't imagine him going there—a place of vulnerability—very often. I hope I'm wrong, but I'm not holding my breath. At least he knows where she stands.

He turns to me. "My wife feels a little bit better about this than I do." His watery eyes go from me to Sophie and then back to me. "It's going to take some time." He raises his chin proudly.

"Whatever happens is okay," I tell him. "As long as I get to be with your granddaughter, everything will be okay."

He gives one nod and leaves, not looking back.

I feel Sophie's rigidity loosening as she eases against me.

"Wow," she says.

"That was interesting," I agree. "Almost as interesting as the flavor of shake I'm about to order for you."

Sophie laughs and presses a kiss to my cheek. "You love my weirdness," she says before kissing me again.

"I do. I love everything about you, Sophie." Now I kiss her cheek, right below her eye.

She tilts her head to meet my gaze, her beautiful brown eyes searching mine.

And at this moment, a truth hits my gut. Home isn't a place at all. My home, in the truest sense of the word, is Sophie Lawson.

Epilogue

Sophie

The third Saturday of August, Present Day

"I'm sure you're right about that," I say to a member of the library board over the phone.

That's right. I said library board. Because now, it's not just little ol' me who's on it. We now have six members, one from each of the towns in Marshall County. Losing Scott in the late spring lit a fire under me. I took matters into my own hands and didn't need to wait for the board to get around to making a decision. I'd had enough of the crappy conditions, enough of the council's dismissal, enough of everything. I went back to fundraising, and this time, instead of earning enough money for an old, broken-down bus, I got enough money over a two-month-long campaign online to finance the purchase and renovation of two buildings, on opposite ends of the county, that can house the libraries.

Scott, may he rest in peace, was the first and hopefully the last of his kind here in Marshall County.

So now, the board meets once a month, and I'm plugging along with the project. We're hoping to open the Longdale location in less than a year, and the Fairhill location on the other side of the county a few months after that.

I end the call and turn to much more enjoyable matters: my boyfriend. I glance over at Oliver, eating his peach pie shake, looking like he's on top of the world.

"You look far too happy for your own good," I chide.

We finish our closing night milkshakes, seal our date with a kiss, and climb in his Mercedes. Before I sit down, I gingerly pick a tuft of Wilford hair off my seat and hide it in my hand. My glance darts to him as I roll the window down to be rid of it in the night air.

"I saw that," he says, his eyes still on the road.

I can't help the laughter that rises up, and he joins in. "I'm sorry," I say. "Wilford's sorry, too! I thought I was being so sneaky."

He only shakes his head as we begin to drive to my house. I don't want this date to end. Because for the first time, he's not leaving town right after our closing night date.

I revel in the thought. I'm in love with this man. And he lives here in Longdale with Alec in that little house on the resort property. We've promised each other that when things at the resort calm down a little, which should be in a month, we'll travel. I'll need to get back eventually to get the libraries ready. That's plural, baby. *Libraries.*

But we can take our time and I can't wait.

He starts to slow to turn onto my street, and I cluck my tongue. "How about we don't go back to my house? Let's just keep driving for a little while."

"Okay?" He glances at me once before returning his gaze on the road. His brow furrows.

My heart starts to pound.

Except for giving him directions on where to turn next, I stay quiet the rest of the way, which is harder than when I had to climb the rope in junior high P.E.

I have so many things to say!

But I refrain from saying a single one of them. He's smiling broadly by the time we pull into the resort, and he parks in the private garage for management. I take his hand, and we walk through the garage to the resort and ride the elevator to the fourth floor.

We say nothing as we walk along the corridor to his office—well, former office. I know he knows by now what this is. Ever since he gave me free reign over turning the office into the resort library, I've had a strict policy: Oliver is not welcome in that room.

It's felt harsh at times, but I've been obsessing over surprising him. These last couple of weeks, I've made a huge push to be done in time for our big, significant date to the shake shop. And with the help of Claire, Alec, Sebastian, and Milo, we did it.

We reach the door, the back of my neck prickling with anticipation. I pull him to a stop, unable to contain my smile.

"Oliver," I say, realizing I'm bouncing up and down slightly. There's no way I can stop it, though.

"Sophie," he says. His face, so handsome and animated, causes me to lose my train of thought a moment. I realize I love him even more than I did yesterday. But how is that even possible?

"Do you know what's about to happen?" I ask him.

"I think so." His gaze glitters. "Do you?"

I scoff. "Yes, I do. Are you ready?"

Without warning he lunges for the door and opens it, then takes a couple of steps inside. "Oliver!" I scream and then start to laugh because his mouth has formed an "O." When he recovers from the surprise, he spins to me. In one swift move, he's lifted me in the air and is holding me in his arms.

I whoop in shock. He cradles me, and I wrap my arms around his neck.

He walks to every point, carrying me in his arms, shaking his head in wonder, telling me he hardly even recognizes the room.

All of the furnishings from before, and even my own office nook, are gone. The walls are lined with floor to ceiling shelves, which contain books and potted plants, even his funny paperweight sits among them to balance the aesthetic. The furniture from the library area is here, too. Plus, there's a child's area with a small table and chair set and even a child's sized bookcase with a small slide.

He turns to the opposite wall, and his gasp is worth all the pain in my tush that this particular item gave me. "There's a sliding ladder?" he asks.

I squirm out of his arms and run to it, shimmying up before he can stop me. "And it's functional, baby!" I'm going so fast that the ladder slides across the upper and lower railings it's connected to. Reaching the top, I finger the books on the highest shelf. I turn to smile at him, but now he's down on one knee, holding a thick, leather-bound book I've never seen before.

Now it's my turn to gasp.

"Sophie? Come here," he says, his eyes pleading.

My heart thuds in my head and ears as I carefully make my way down the ladder. How did my surprise for him turn into this?

"You okay?" he asks tenderly.

I nod. I'm suddenly out of breath. "When a man's on one knee holding a book, I find it extra hard to think clearly."

He laughs and that's when his serious expression melts away.

"How?" I ask, placing my hand over his hand resting on the top of the book. "Wait a second." I suddenly go rigid. "Did your brothers show you this already?"

"No, I promise you, they did not." His expression is grave. "But they may have let it slip that you were trying to have it done by today, so I decided to work on a surprise of my own. They hid this in here for me today."

Never one to delay things, he opens the book, holding the bottom half as the top cover falls away to reveal not pages, but a small square safe.

"I know you were probably hoping this was a real book," Oliver says. He's alive with energy, and his eyes are dancing.

"I kind of was," I admit, grinning so hard my mouth hurts.

He surveys the room. "I think we have enough real books in here for now."

"There's no such thing as enough books, but—" I lick my lips and shake my head. This is happening right now. I need to stop talking and let the man speak.

He pops open the safe to reveal a ring box.

My ankles feel weak. I nod to encourage him to ask the question I've wanted to say yes to for so long.

"I love you more than anything or anyone," he says, his voice trembling. "Sophie, will you be by my side forever? Will you be my wife?"

I laugh out a yes even before he's opened the ring box. But my laugh turns into a squeal when I see the rock: an emerald-cut white diamond center stone with a delicate, glittering band.

I drop to my knees next to him, set the ring box and fake book aside, and clutch his face in my hands. "Yes," I say more strongly this time. "I love you." He slides the ring on my finger and we kiss, the scent of paper pages and bindings, old and new, in the air.

Read the love story of Sophie's coworker, Violet and her handsome, yet grumpy, traveling companion, Hayden, in *Just a Road Trip* for FREE by joining my newsletter!

Read about Oliver's brother, Alec, next in *Just a Football Star.*

Check out the first chapter of Alec's story on the next page.

Chapter 1 of Just a Football Star

Oakley

I need a gigantic bag of chocolate-covered cinnamon bears like I need air. Maybe slightly more.

I step up to the front desk of the Tate International Longdale Lake Resort, imagining a bag that is truly jumbo-sized, the kind you can get at the candy factory's outlet store.

Don't ask me how I know.

So what if the bears' faces are malformed, or the chocolate looks a little lumpy? I don't need my candy to look pretty, okay? I need it to do its job.

Why didn't I think to grab one from the store before I left San Antonio?

Oh. That's right. I was a little distracted by the fog of broken-heartedness, lack of funds, and an inability to conjure up any sense of space and time.

Slinging my bag that doubles as a laptop carry-on and holder of the essentials from my life back home higher on my shoulder, I realize the guy at the front desk is talking to me.

"Can you repeat the question?" I offer an artificial laugh. I've been on an adrenaline bender the last couple of days—not by choice—and the afterburn has rendered me nearly useless. Which is why I should either go for a run to clear my head or eat spicy candy to numb it. And let's face it. The candy sounds much more appealing right now.

"Oh, I was only welcoming you to Longdale. First time here?" The front desk guy's grin feels genuine—like he's happy to be at work today.

I raise my hand like I'm in grade school. "First timer!"

He smiles and looks at his computer screen, then clicks his tongue. "It looks like your room isn't ready yet. I apologize. You're welcome to hang out in the lobby for an hour or so until housekeeping's finished." He sweeps his hand across my line of vision to highlight the high-end luxurious space with cozy lighting, carved fireplaces, and rich leathers. "And I can get you a water and a granola bar while you wait."

I shake my head. Sitting in a lobby feels vulnerable right now. I might actually have to talk to people.

"You don't have another room available that I could switch to? I don't mind two queen beds."

Sympathy stirs behind his eyes. "I'm sorry, but no. We're at full capacity right now."

I sigh and chew on my lip. This fits my new life. It's a life that could be called "Everything's Impossible."

It's impossible to do such things as crash in my hotel room after a sleepless night. Or quit a job gracefully. Or have a man in your life who you can trust to clean up after himself and do such things as, I don't know, *not* steal from you.

□At least the resort is nice, with its old-world-rustic-meets-fancy-castle style. Lizzy, my coworker—now former coworker—said it's only been open for a few months. It still smells new. The AC cools my clammy skin.

□I tell him it's fine and that I'll check back with him in an hour. It takes all my energy to stay civil, but I do. Just because my life is in the dumpster doesn't mean I have to lose all sense of politeness.

□I turn from the counter and glance out the double doors to see the early afternoon, azure, June sky with a puffy cloudscape. The resort seems to be built right into the steep mountainside, providing up-close views of the natural lake. The scene is a painting—like it's not real.

Normally, I'd go dip my toes and skip rocks along the water. But not now. I have zero plans to venture out. I'm going to hole up in my room. Of course, I'll still wake up at five because I've been doing that for years. I'll stick to my workout routine because I don't know how to be a human without that.

But I'll also breathe, order room service, and eventually emerge only to scrounge up some chocolate-covered cinnamon bears—Longdale better have them. And then sleep. And then order more room service.

□If it's not too pricey. I shunt out a hot breath as I remember, with a jolt, that I'm suddenly on a tight budget. With no income right now, I have to be. I haven't had to cut back for a long time. That was one of the perks of my job as a senior trainer for the San Antonio Wolves, the NFL team I'd spent the last ten months working for. I had enough money for my needs and then some.

□No more. None of that exists for me now.

Somehow I have the wherewithal to scrounge up the desire to go running. I return to the front desk. "You have a gym, right?" I seem to remember reading mention of one through the fuzzy rage-booking I did the night before.

"Yes. Construction was just completed last week—the final phase of the resort." He gestures to his right along a corridor paved in cream tile. "It's down past the elevators and conference rooms."

I thank him and turn to leave, declining his offer to keep my stuff back behind the desk for me. No, thank you. Ever since my life imploded two days ago, I've felt this need to curl into myself. Letting my bags out of my sight feels ridiculously unsafe.

It doesn't make any sense, but I can't argue with it.

I find the gym and it's one of the best I've seen. They even have a TechnoGym Kinesis, with oak wall bars and chrome pulleys. It's brand-new exercise tech. Whoever designed this space knew what they were doing. I go in the bathroom and change into my shorts, tank top, and running shoes.

Thankfully, the gym is still unoccupied when I get out. I stow my bag near the treadmill furthest from the door, say a silent prayer that I'll be allowed to run in peace, and jump on. My pace is higher than I normally start out at, but it's like all the pent-up emotion of the last forty-eight hours has to go somewhere. It's not until I've finished the first mile that I realize I don't even have my earbuds in. Totally not my style to run without music, but hey, it's not my style to scurry away from my dream job without a single plan in mind, either.

When Lizzy suggested yesterday that I go to Colorado to get away from the fallout of discovering my boyfriend was stealing from me, I jumped on it. She said the lakeside Tate resort was peaceful, with opportunities for recreation and sun. Out of the way enough to be alone, but nice enough to feel pampered.

All prerequisites considering that this now ex-boyfriend also works for the Wolves and is the boss's son.

I'm beginning my third mile when a man walks into the gym. Great. Just what I needed. He's tall with dark hair and nicely sculpted thighs and calves. He's pretty much Adonis in every way, physically speaking. And I mean that in a professional, medical way, only.

Except, I'm not a trainer—not anymore. Swallowing down *that* lovely pain, I focus on my own running. From the looks of him, he's probably here to lift weights anyway. I'll ignore him and if I'm lucky, he'll ignore me, too.

Nope. No such luck. He's getting on the treadmill right next to me. Really, dude? There's another one. A perfectly good one that looks as nice and new as the others, at the end of the row. Why choose this one? He obviously doesn't understand gym etiquette.

I increase my speed by one-tenth and train my focus on the video of trees that the treadmill is simulating for me. Yeah. Just focus on the trees, not the totally hot but inconsiderate guy running next to you.

It doesn't take me long to realize his strides are matching my own, and there's something familiar about him. I hazard a glance in his direction, and it's like he'd been waiting for me to look over.

"Hey," he says, bobbing his head once.

I give a slight nod and then focus on my pseudo forest. I don't say hey back because I'm out of breath. But that doesn't mean my body isn't affected by his handsome face and body. His lateral muscles are defined, the jagged edges of his scapula visible under his tight t-shirt.

Again, I'm only noticing because it's been my job to notice such things—you know, the musculature of athletes. And it's obvious he's athletic, and that I've seen him before.

"Did you just get here at the resort today?" he asks. "Or have you been here awhile?"

Mr. Chatty Charlie needs to stop. Who even does that? Starts talking to someone who's clearly in the zone?

I offer a brief, tight smile. "First day." I feel compelled to return the question. "How about you?" I ask between breaths.

He hesitates. "I've been here awhile."

I nod and then turn the speed up again. Maybe he'll get the hint that I need him to leave me alone if he sees that I'm trying to go faster.

I don't miss that he does the same, and one glance at his console tells me he's matched my speed exactly. The thing is, he's taller than me by several inches, which means he can match me with little effort.

I give it another few seconds and then turn up my speed again. I'm close to the maximum I'm willing to do and sweat is starting to bead at my forehead. This was supposed to be a run to kill the time, not PR. *Come on.* I growl internally.

A glance in his direction rewards me because I see the smug grin on his face starting to dissipate. He's breathing heavily now and sweating, too. For someone as obviously fit as he is, his lung capacity is weirdly low.

And he *is* fit—an athlete. He's in good shape, but the way he's running tells me maybe he's taken a hiatus from working out recently. His steps are unnaturally labored. And the fact that he's an athlete sobers me—it reminds me to be careful.

I can't let the guy beat me, so I notch my speed up a little higher, and he does the same. Who is he and why is he so insecure that he has to be running faster than me?

Oh well. It's his funeral. I can stay in my lane. I press the button three more times for good measure. I know I can do it. It's not what I wanted to do, but I'll survive another few minutes at this pace. It's a very good thing I haven't had my chocolate-covered cinnamon bear binge yet.

After a few moments, he's sucking wind and if I'm being honest, so am I. This is hard. Darn you, you good looking man who I may or may not know from somewhere and who may or may not be a sexist pig trying to one up me because I'm a woman.

At the five-mile mark, my ankle wobbles and for one brief moment, I imagine myself slipping on the treadmill belt and going down hard. Whoa, whoa, whoa. I've got to focus here. I press my palm against my head for a few steps to regain control. Sweat trickles down my back and my hair slips from my ponytail.

But focusing doesn't mean letting down. I may die at the thought of increasing my speed by even one more tenth of a mile, but I can keep going a little longer at this pace. My hamstrings and calves are screaming for relief. I could stop. His run has been way shorter than mine, anyway, so I've already won.

Then, why can't I push the stop button? I know I'm competitive—a trait that has gotten me where I am today. I'm proud of that.

Except, with a dash of pain, I remember that where I am today—like, actually today—unemployed, unboyfriended, and exquisitely unhappy, is nothing to be proud of.

□My fingers hover over the big, red STOP button, my lungs are on fire, the lactic acid in my muscles making each cell scream. Just as I reach out to push it, I hear a sleek whistle of belt against metal, a screech of gears, and a thunk, thunk of falling bones and muscles.

□To my horror, Chatty Charlie is sprawled on the ground behind me.

To continue reading, click below:

https://www.amazon.com/dp/B0C9Q261WJ

Just a FOOTBALL Star

DEB GOODMAN

Author's Note

I had so much fun writing this book! It took over a year to write because it was the first time I'd ventured into the Romantic Comedy genre, first person point of view, and present tense. It was all just...a lot...of new stuff going on. But with the help of an army of people, it's here!

Cameron, thank you for coming up with Sophie's dog's name, Wilford. It's perfect for him.

Linda, you saved me, yet again, from so many blunders. Your insight and friendship are vital to me.

Britney, Lori, Maren, Terra, and Lindzee, your beta reading saved this book from itself—from the hot mess it once was. Thank you.

Gigi, thank you for the beautiful, beautiful cover. It is a work of art.

To all of my ARC readers and the Bookstagram community: Thank you from the bottom of my heart. You are all amazing individuals.

Vanessa, Sam, Cameron, and Max (as well as the rest of my family), I love you. Thanks for being so supportive of my books.

David, you are my true companion. Thank you for helping me come up with cool names, jokes, and details (like the shake shop's name: Shake,

Shake, Shake). Thank you for your kindness in listening to me vent about what a hard gig this writer life can be sometimes. And thank you for loving my dreams, rooting for me, and being by my side. I love you.

About the Author

Deb Goodman's obsession with the written word started at age three, when she realized the old-timey newsprint wallpaper in her family's bathroom had actual words on it. The only problem? By the time she learned to read a couple of years later, the wallpaper had been replaced with something else—boring, non-worded wallpaper—and to this day, she still doesn't know what it said.

Now, she and her husband and four children live in Utah. They love sports, music, and doing slightly insulting, pretend voices for their little shorkie, Mavis.

Deb writes funny, small-town romance that you won't need to shield your kids' eyes from. Billionaires, friends-to-more, enemies-to-more, cowboys, fake relationships...there's something for everyone here!

Writing lovey dovey books comes naturally to Deb since, to her, there's nothing better than reading and writing about how two people fall in love.

Connect with her!

Newsletter: https://bit.ly/3DtjNSU

or visit https://debgoodmanwrites.com

Amazon: https://www.amazon.com/stores/Deb-Goodman/author/B07L4YL1CL

Instagram: https://instagram.com/debgoodmanwrites

TikTok handle: @debgoodmanauthor

Facebook: https://www.facebook.com/debgoodmanwrites

BookBub: https://www.bookbub.com/authors/deb-goodman

Website: https://debgoodmanwrites.com